FERAL
crown

AN AGE GAP ROMANCE

ELEANOR ALDRICK

For my Warr;ors.

You are worthy.
You are enough.
You are loved.

If you or anyone you know is struggling with depression, please know that it isn't a weakness to ask for help.

You are not alone.

ON REPEAT Playlist

Do I Move You - **Nina Simone**
La Noche De Anoche - Bad Bunny & ROSALIA
Cover Me Up - **Morgan Wallen**
Deeper Than the Holler - Randy Travis
You Make it Easy - **Jason Aldean**
People You Know - Selena Gomez
Yikes - **Nicki Minaj**
Watch Me Glow - DOLLA
If He Wanted to He Would - **Kylie Morgan**
Tennessee Whiskey - Chris Stapleton
Rock and A Hard Place - **Bailey Zimmerman**
Make You Feel - Alina Baraz & Galimatias
If you Want Love - **NF**
Watergate - Madchild
Hrs & Hrs - **Muni Long**

Prologue
MELISSA

It's all fucked. *What's the point?* Besides, it's not like I'll be missed.

Whatever. I'm doing it. At least then, I won't feel. And this incessant ache? It'll finally be gone.

My decision made, I dig my bare feet into the pine needles and leaves scattered beneath me—my own personal runway into freedom. Freedom from this dark abyss that threatens to take me under. *Every. Damn. Day.*

God, I'm tired. *So damn tired.*

Like a siren's call, the wind beats against my face. *She's telling me it's time.*

And as if in answer, my heart picks up its beat, helping me realize that this is the most alive I've felt in ages. Good. I welcome it. Right along with the pain from the branches now piercing my soles.

With every stride forward, my body gains speed, and that's when I see it—the cliff's edge.

Feet carry me into the light, where I may finally breathe and be free. A little longer. Just a few more steps.

But because life is nothing but cruel, my relief is denied and I'm forced back down into the pain of this world by a large body blindsiding my own.

I'm knocked onto my ass, the scattered twigs now digging into my back, reminding me that I'm still on this torturous plane.

"Maverick," I grunt, barely able to breathe as his large body smothers me.

"What the fuck, Melissa! What in-the-actual-fuck were you thinking?!" My brother's best friend finally peels himself off my small frame, but only enough to assess my face—for what? I have no clue.

I say nothing. There's nothing *to* say.

"Answer me, little girl or I'll drag your scrawny ass right to your brother and tell him what I found you doing."

My eyes narrow, face scrunching up right before I bust out in hysterical laughter—all while this massive man straddles me, as if his body weight will keep me from flying off the cliff not ten feet away.

"You," I cackle, "you think…" more uncontrollable

laughter, "You think that telling my brother is going to scare me? I was just about to plummet into darkness, and you think that ratting me out will get me talking?"

Deep amber eyes blink down at me, and I see Maverick is at a loss for words—which isn't saying much. This is the most he's said to me in the five years I've known him. He's a loner and his only friend is my brother, another recluse. I swear, they'd be happy holed up in the woods for months at a time, not giving a damn about the world around them.

Finally, something registers on his face and his bulky frame eases back. I'm thinking he's about to leave me in my state of hysteria—I'm too much for anyone to deal with, let alone someone like him—but his next actions surprise the hell out of me. He drags me onto his lap, his massive arms wrapping around me as he brings my head to his chest with one hand while the other grips my lithe body to his.

And on a harsh whisper, Maverick delivers the words that will forever change my trajectory on this fucked up planet.

"Now you listen to me, and you listen to me good." His chest rises with a deep inhale before his next words fall on the exhale. "Life isn't perfect. Far from it. At times, it can be absolutely devastating and downright painful. But that isn't the constant and it isn't what we should hang onto... You see, life is like a rollercoaster, and just as deeply as you feel these lows—I promise you, baby doll—the highs will be equally as breathtaking and worth every fucking second of the hell you endured to get there."

My chest is so heavy right now, my throat tight. I can't help it. All of the darkness inside of me pours out, my eyes burning with the onslaught of tears raining down my cheeks and onto Mav's shirt.

"Ssshhhh, baby. It'll be okay. You'll find your light, I promise." His calloused grip drops to my neck and squeezes. "Once you feel how good life can be, you'll cling onto those moments with all you hold dear. Those moments, as small and as fleeting as they are, they're worth living for."

Maverick presses his lips to my temple, the action making my ugly sobs now come out in full force. "No. They're not for me. I can't feel them. I never have."

"You just haven't been listening, baby doll." Strong hands grip my biceps and turn me until I'm straddling this strange feral version of Buddha. "Dig your toes into the ground and close your eyes, feeling the ground beneath you." I do as he says and once he's satisfied, he squeezes my hips and continues. "Okay, now take in a deep breath and feel the coolness entering your body, filling it with energy…" Once again, I comply, and once again, I get a little squeeze of assurance. "Good girl, now exhale and let all that darkness out."

My heart gallops in place. These seemingly small things filling me with curiosity for more.

"This. You will always have this. No matter how fucked

up life is around you, you'll always have the earth to ground you. Take it. Use it. Let it center you and help you find your focus. Come out of it stronger and show that situation who the fuck is boss." Pillowy lips press to my forehead and a shiver runs through me. Something I've never felt before, and I'd be lying if I said I wasn't hungry for more. "You're the boss, baby doll. Go grab life by the balls and make it your bitch."

"Make life my bitch," I mumble into Maverick's shirt, repeating my newfound mantra.

I have no clue how this man managed to turn me upside down in a matter of minutes, but for someone who's spoken all but two words to me before, he's sure as hell made up for the lack of communication just now.

Begrudgingly, I pull back. "Okay." Wiping at my tear-stained face, I feel a stream of snot drip out of my nose. *Thank you, Life. You fucking bitch.* With a pointed index finger, I shove at his hard chest. "But just so you know. If I don't find these moments you speak of, I'm holding you personally accountable."

Maverick throws his head back, his throaty chuckle lighting up every part of my body and flooding me with confusing emotions. "Deal, baby doll. Deal."

This has my brows reaching up toward my hairline. "So quick to make a deal with the devil I see. You do know that if I come after you, I'm dragging both of us over that cliff?"

My new life coach continues to chuckle as he lifts us off the ground, never missing a beat as he throws me over his shoulder before punctuating his sentence with a swat to my ass. "I'd like to see you try, little girl. I'd tie you up before you even got to step a foot into these woods."

Holy fuck. He was being playful but the thoughts that popped up into my head were anything but. I'm talking about Fifty Shades of Broody Mountain Man... and I'm not mad at it. *Nope.* I'm hungry for more.

"Now, let's go see about moving you out of that shithole. There's no way I'm letting you go back with Bruce after that stunt you pulled. If your father isn't going to be watching out for you, then I'll make sure Ericson is."

My body freezes at his words. He's right. There's no way I could go back home, but I'm not moving in with my brother. He's a park ranger and sharing a tiny cabin with that slob is already giving me the itch to run.

As a matter of fact...

"Not. Happening." I wiggle with all that I have, managing to find a ticklish spot on the beast of a man. *Jackpot. His weakness.* One I exploit until he's dropping me like a hot potato, the small move causing him to stumble.

With as much speed as I can muster, I rise up and run—run as fast as my battered feet can carry me. *Thank you, Clover High Track Team.* Who knew those skills would come in so handy.

"What the fuck, Mel!" He's howling behind me but I'm not stopping. I'll find my own way out of this, and it definitely isn't going to be shacking up with my brother.

And as the road comes into view, I see her. My classmate, Koko. *Technically Mila Kournikova, but they call her Koko for short.*

Perfect.

With a boost of energy I didn't know I had, I dash toward the car and notice the older version of her behind the wheel. Her eyes are glassed over as she talks on the phone, but I don't even stop to think before wrenching the rear passenger door open and jumping inside.

"Melissa?" She looks down at my crouched position on the floorboards, her mother oblivious to what's going on behind her or not even caring.

I whisper-shout. "Turn back around! My brother's best friend is about to pop out of those woods. If he asks, you haven't seen me."

Mila nods, her petite frame turning to face the road as her hand drops a large coat over the back—the perfect cover from nosy mountain men.

She doesn't owe me anything, nor do I have anything to give her. This small act of kindness is all her, and I'd be lying if I said it didn't warm my chest, loosening some of the bitterness I hold inside.

Mila is doing *me* a solid. Just because she can. *I think I love her already.*

And as I hear the window roll down and my new best friend cover for me, I know that I really do. But more than that, I've finally found it. My first moment of light in this fucked up world.

Chapter One
MELISSA

THREE YEARS LATER

"You're bat shit Crazy, Mel." My best friend of over two years is looking at me as if I've just grown a second head.

"Not crazy. More like… *determined*."

"Determined to catch a disease," she mumbles under her breath as she shuffles through the outfits I've laid out in the small loft. "The waitress uniforms are scandalous enough as it is. And these? You're bound to catch a VD just by walking into The Pearl with this. They don't even cover your hoo-haw!"

"That's the point, genius. How am I supposed to get the job of a dancer if I go in looking like Mother Mary?" I snatch the little black number from her fingers, quickly sliding it over my naked body. "If I want the job of a seductress, I have to look the part of a seductress. Besides, you're the seasoned veteran here. Had it not been for your connection, I wouldn't have gotten the interview."

My friend rolls her eyes. "Trust me, Mel. You don't want the job of a dancer. Yes, they make more money than I do, but the guys are downright sleazeballs. You'd be much happier serving drinks with me."

I balance on one leg as I slide on a platform stiletto. "Negative, Ryder. I'm not doing this for the money. Although I appreciate how much you've been bringing in and it helping us get a car and all."

"Okay. I get it. Not about the money. You're trying to get Maverick to lose his shit when he sees you." She blows out a long breath as she plops backward onto the bed. "But do you have to go to such extremes? If you get caught using a fake ID to get this job, then you'll be in deep shit. At least with me, nobody cares enough to raise a stink. But as soon as Maverick finds out, he's liable to burn the whole place to the ground, and then we'll both be out of a job."

"I'm eighteen. If anyone gets in trouble, it'll be on me. Even so, I doubt Mav would risk putting me behind bars." My stomach does a somersault as I say this.

It doesn't matter. My crush is going out of town soon and I'd definitely be willing to risk a little jail time.

The past three years have been an insane roller coaster of confusing emotions, but one thing has remained constant. My need for one particularly stoic man. But despite the hints that I've more than liberally sprinkled in front of my brother's best friend, he's never taken the bait. Never once showed any interest.

Well, that changes tonight.

Maverick doesn't react to much, but one thing I can count on is his overprotectiveness. *Lucky me.* He won't date me, but he sure as hell doesn't have a problem being my warden.

Ever since that day at the cliff, Maverick has been a permanent installment in my life. Even helped me find the tiny home I now share with Mila—said he knew the landlord and helped us work out a deal that even I could afford. Sure, Mila makes more since she stopped working at the diner with me, but that's also why this gig at The Pearl is so perfect. She needs the money and I need a Thelma to my Louise.

"Hey, aren't you tired of carrying most of the financial weight around here? Just think about it. Me up-leveling to a dancer…" Looking down at my best friend's disapproving eyes, I give her my best saleswoman spiel. "You, up-leveling to a—"

At this she sits up, her hands frantically waving in front of her. "Oh no. I know where you're going with this and I'm not going to be a part of it. I can't dance to save my life. I'd just make a fool of myself, and you know it."

I cackle. She's right. Girl has two left feet, bless her heart. "Oh, I would *never* suggest you be a dancer." A pillow comes flying at me, but I swat it away. "Hey, I'm not trying to be mean, but you're right and I totally wasn't suggesting you be a dancer.... but behind the bar? Totally doable. Doable and a heck of a lot more money than waitressing, so you've said."

Mila throws her head back and lets out a full bellied laugh. "Using a fake ID to waitress versus using it to bartend? Yeah. There's a huge difference. Money be damned. I'm not going to jail."

"Okay, so maybe it's a gamble. But the money is still better, and you do need that."

Mila slowly nods, her face scrunching up that way it does when she's in deep thought. "Actually. I think I have a plan."

"Oh, this is good. You've got that look." I grab the pillow off the ground and sit on the bed next to her, giving her shoulder a small shove. "Spill it."

"Okay, but no judging." She raises a brow, and now it's my turn to hit her with the pillow.

"Girl, you know I never do. Not even that one time you ended up peeing your pants because we didn't make it up the mountain in time." I purse my lips, my mind flitting back to before we had our Civic and the bus stop was a good two miles away from our house.

"You swore you wouldn't talk about that ever again!" Mila swats at me and squeals.

I cackle, palms up. "Okay. Okay. My bad. But seriously, get to spilling."

Mila bites the corner of her lip before shocking the ever-living-shit out of me. "I'm auctioning off my virginity."

My mouth must hang open a solid minute before I finally get the wherewithal to form a sentence. "I'm sorry. Come again? You *never* talk to men. I mean, like, never. And here you are thinking of offering your kitty up on a silver platter? Why?"

"You said it. I need the money." She shrugs as if this is the most logical thing ever.

"Yeah. So work behind the bar. Sure, it's a risk, but it's better than giving your cherry away to some random stranger." My brows push together as I try to figure out how long she's been planning this for.

Mila faces me before she's clamping her hands down on my shoulders. "You know I'd never do anything without hashing and rehashing all of the pros and cons, right? Well, one little night eclipses bartending money tenfold. And bonus, there's no risk of jail time." I nod but can't add much more. I'm still in shock from this bombshell. "Look, I'm sick and tired of having no control over my life. The way I see it, I'm taking life by the balls like you always say. This way, it's me who's in charge. I'm going to lose it anyway. Might as well get something useful out of it."

"Mila. You can't be serious." I shake my head and laugh, but there's no humor in it. "One day, you're going to meet the love of your life, and that experience you share with him will be worth ten times over whatever some joe schmo will pay."

My friend scoffs. "We can't all be as lucky as you, Melissa. It's not like some Knight in shining armor is going to save me from certain death."

I roll my eyes, fully getting the dig. "Maverick doesn't want me, so that doesn't really count. Besides, this is my last-ditch effort. If this doesn't work, then I'm moving out of state. There's no sense in me staying around when you're leaving for college and that man doesn't even see me."

Mila looks me over, her eyebrows wagging. "Oh, he sees you. Just not in the way you want...*yet*. But as soon as he gets an eyeful of this, he's going to pounce. I'm sure of it."

"Yeah. Well, I don't have your confidence." I fling myself back onto the bed as a deep sigh leaves my lips. "And I mean it. I'm leaving if this doesn't work."

Mila snorts. "Girl, you know I support you in everything you do—even this hair-brained scheme to dance at The Pearl—but you and I both know that as long as that man lives and breathes, your ass is staying right here in Colorado."

She's right. It would take something pretty drastic for me to give up on Maverick. *Still.* I'll never beg a man for attention. *Nope.* I'll just have to make myself hard-as-fuck to ignore.

Hunter, Two months later...

"Bro, when are you coming back?" Matt's worried voice cuts through the receiver and the hair on the back of my neck stands at attention.

"I'll be home tomorrow. What's the problem?"

"Nothing I can put my finger on, but Jack's acting weird and I just know something's up." Matt sighs and I can practically hear his wheels turning.

We may be twins, but we are different in every way possible. Matt is polished, and I'm not. Matt over analyzes everything, and I *do not*.

"You sure you aren't making mountains out of molehills again? The last time you thought something was going on it turned out to be nothing more than your cleaning lady having changed the laundry detergent on you."

"I don't appreciate your tone, brother. And I'll have you know that shit makes a difference." Matt huffs to the sound of papers shuffling in the background. "Listen, I know how much you hate it when my mind plays 'what if,' but Austin's a lovesick fool and Jace just left for Florida—so that leaves me with you."

"Fine. Lay it on me."

"Well. You already know shit hasn't been the same since our parents passed. One thing after another and we still don't really know what happened."

Oh, I know what happened. Our family got mixed up

with rival cartels long ago, and the fallout of everything is still with us 'til this day.

"And? I thought we all agreed to leave that up to the men of WRATH securities. Don't tell me you've been digging up shit on your own."

Silence. Nothing but silence.

"Matt?"

"Yeah. Well, the men of WRATH aren't moving fast enough so I thought I'd help them along."

I roll my eyes. *They aren't moving fast enough because I'm paying them not to.* But I can't tell Matt that. I can't tell any of my brothers, though I suspect Jack knows.

"Alright. So what trouble are you getting into?"

"Get this… I was at the Pearl the other day—hey, did you know Ericson's little sister is working there now? Anyway—"

Matt keeps talking but all I hear is the sound of my heart pounding in my ears. Did he just say Mel is working at *the Pearl*? The Pearl. A fucking strip joint.

I leave for three goddamn months, needing to distance myself from the girl that's sure to ruin me, only to have her turn around and get into trouble the first chance she gets?

Fucking bullshit.

"Bro? Hey, bro? Are you there?" Matt calls to me, but it sounds as if he's underwater. Or maybe that's just me, drowning in this rage I have no business feeling.

"Yeah, I'm sorry. I just remembered I have something I need to be doing. Can this wait until tomorrow?"

"Um, sure. Just drop by before you head up to the cabin. We can break into the first batch of the season." Keys click in the background letting me know he's already moved on and thank God. I don't have the mental fortitude to go through one of his rabbit holes.

"Alright. See you tomorrow." I cut the line and quickly dial the town's Sheriff. With the population of thirty, there isn't much Spence doesn't have his finger on.

Two rings and there's an answer. "Well, I'll be. It's Hunter Crown, gracing me with a call. To what do I owe the pleasure?"

I'm rolling my eyes for the second time in an hour. "Don't act like we never talk, Spence. I just saw you before leaving town."

He chuckles into the receiver. "I'm just busting your balls, man. Usually I'm the one who has to track you down, see if you're up for some hunting or fishing. Anyway, what can I do you for?"

"Melissa. Ericson's little sister."

"Hmm." There's a hint of amusement in his tone and I wonder if he already knows. "What about her?"

"She still working at the diner?" My heart beats overtime waiting on his answer, knowing that whatever he says has the power to sway my mood like a goddamn pendulum.

"No, sir. Can't say that I've seen her at Poppy's since you left."

Full. On. Rage.

"And you didn't think to tell me?!"

"Woah, there, buddy. It ain't my job to be her babysitter or your damn secretary. You're the one who took on the job of her guardian, not me, so don't you go putting that business where it don't belong."

He's right. Of course he's right. But I can't help it when it comes to her. Spencer is the only one who knows of my obsession with keeping that girl safe—something I've never shared with anyone, not even her brother. Hell, the only reason Spencer knows is because he caught me trailing Mel and her roommate home one night, and it took me two whole months to convince him I wasn't some sort of sick pervert praying on the girls.

"Okay. My bad." Clearing my throat, I try to regain some of my composure, but it isn't easy. Not when all I can think of is Mel being ogled by sleazy men.

Just then, a vision of her tight ass being groped flashes before me, and I swear I feel a blood vessel pop.

"I know the cabin is out of your jurisdiction, but I don't get in until the morning. Do you mind driving by her place tonight and making sure she's okay?"

Spence chuckles. "Of course, friend. But you owe me."

I sigh into the line. "Just tell me which property and it's yours for a week."

"Opalaka lake house. I've got this girl I want to impress."

Now it's my turn to laugh. "Oh, this is good. I've never seen you with anyone more than once, and you're wanting to take a girl up there for *a whole week*? She must be special."

"Oh, she's special alright. Got my tail wagging and head spinning just like you with that Ericson girl."

At this, my mood sours. "It isn't like that, Spence. You already know that."

"No, friend. I don't. Seems like you're the only one telling yourself that lie."

"It isn't a lie. She's my friend's sister and way too young. She isn't for me." I run a hand through my hair, tugging at the ends in frustration. "Look, just message me when you know she's okay."

"Sure thing, buddy." Spencer chuckles as he cuts the line and I'm glad to be rid of him. I've already got one psychoanalyzer in the family, *I don't need another.*

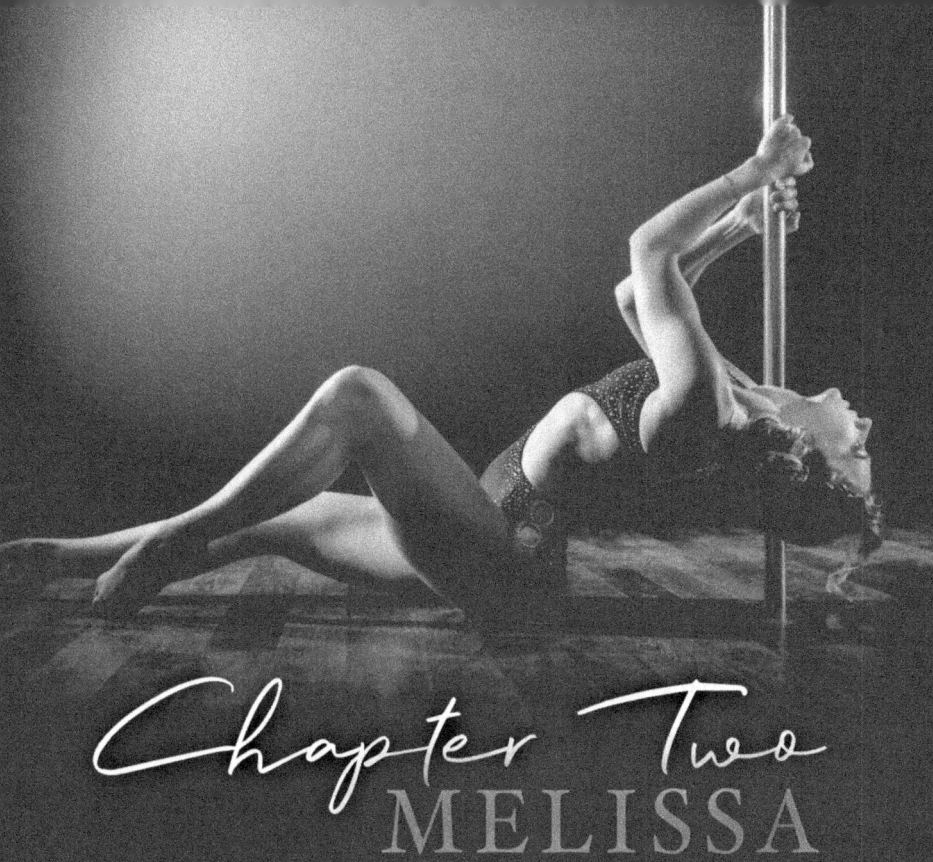

Chapter Two
MELISSA

"You're up next, doll!" The head dancer calls out to me as I finish up my makeup.

It's been three months since I started working here, and even though this gig started off as a ploy to ruffle mavericks feathers, I quite enjoy what I do. There's this heady sense of empowerment, being able to bring men to their knees with just a little wiggle and shake.

"I'm coming!" I turn toward the door, ready to hit the stage but I hit a hard chest instead.

"Like fuck you are." Maverick growls down at me, his thick fingers digging into my naked waist and making a full-bodied shiver wrack through me. I realize I'm wearing no more than underwear in front of the man that's plagued my dreams for as long as I can remember, and my body has definitely taken notice.

"Mav?" His name comes out a soft whisper, I'm surprised he can even hear it.

"Don't you *Mav* me." His grip tightens around me as he pulls me harder into his towering frame. "What the fuck is this, Mel?"

Maverick's eyes move behind me as he survey's the changing room, clearly displeased with what he sees.

"Hey. You aren't supposed to be back here!" I whisper-shriek, trying to wiggle out of his hold, but he isn't having it.

"Answer me, Melissa. What are you doing here?" His piercing eyes find mine and I'm immobilized, turning into the puddle of mush he always manages to make me.

"Working. I'm working." I stare back at him defiantly, unwilling to back down.

He scoffs, his chest vibrating so close to my lips I'm tempted to lean in and kiss it. "No. You aren't. Not anymore." His hands fall from my waist and trail down to my hips before he turns me around and pushes me toward the vanity I'd just left. "Get your shit. We're leaving."

"Oh, no. I'm not." Now that I'm not engulfed in his scent and can finally think again, I've regained my senses. "This is my job, Maverick. I can't just leave. You heard Candy. I'm up next."

I swear I hear my crush outright growl before I'm being hoisted in the air, my body being cradled bridal style as we make it past the vanity and toward the rear exit. "Fuck your things, I can get them later."

Instinctively, my arms wrap around Maverick's thick shoulders before I'm registering what he's just said. "Hold up! I can't just leave!"

"You can, and you are."

"Hey! You don't get to decide that! You aren't my father!" I'm beating on his chest now, trying to get him to slow down, but it's having no effect.

"Yes, I do. I may not be your father, but you clearly need a Daddy." He's staring straight ahead, eyes laser focused on the door.

"Maverick! No!" I give his chest one hard shove. "You don't get to abandon me and then come in here and call the shots."

We stop so fast I'm surprised we haven't hit some invisible barrier.

"Abandoned you?" Maverick is finally looking down at me, his eyes incredulous. "What on God's green earth makes you think I've abandoned you?"

My face heats at this realization. Truth be told, I wasn't even aware I felt that way. But I guess it makes sense.

Sighing, I sink back into his hold, pressing my cheek against a rock-hard pectoral that has me almost forgetting I'm mad. *Almost.*

"You left me. What else would you call it? For three

years, you've trailed me like a second shadow, and then a couple of months ago you vanished without so much as a goodbye."

His body stiffens beneath me, and I know I've hit a nerve. *Good.*

"I had some business to handle. But it doesn't matter. I'm here now."

I scrunch my face, hating that it bothers me so much. I shouldn't care. Shouldn't be hung up on this guy who clearly only sees me as a burden.

I'm about to tell him that it does matter. That he isn't my keeper and that I can make my own decisions when the door to the outside opens and one of the bouncers steps in.

"Mel—" Looking back I see it's Johnny, and by the color of his face I can see he isn't thrilled. "What the fuck is this? You know boyfriends aren't allowed back here."

"I'm not—"

"We're not—"

Mav and I go to answer at the same time, our befuddled responses only serving to cause Johnny more concern if his raised brow and clenching jaw are any indication.

"Someone better answer me quick, or I'm about to beat this man's ass."

"I'd like to see you fuckin' try," Mav growls as his fingers dig deeper into my flesh, his body going rigid next to mine.

"Hey, hey. There's no need for dick measuring." Needing to prevent a fight, I step in—well, as much as my current position allows. "Mav was just about to leave, right?"

I look back at my captor, eyes narrowing, willing him to agree. But of course, he doesn't.

"Only way I'm leaving is with you, baby doll." He raises a brow, not giving a shit that my nails are digging into his *very muscular* traps right now.

"Yeah. That's not going to work." Johnny stares Maverick down as he takes one step closer. "She's needed on stage."

"*She* doesn't work here anymore."

"Maverick!" I shriek, slapping at his chest with the palm of my hand. "You can't say that! I'll lose my job!"

"Good." The one word comes out more of a grunt than English, but it comes out clear enough for Johnny to hear.

"I don't think she's in agreement with you, so I suggest you put her down."

"I won't be doing that, so I suggest you get out of my way."

"That's not happening." Before I can fully assess what's going on, Johnny moves to rip me out of Maverick's arms.

A bad move. My brother's best friend has always been a force to be reckoned with, but now? He seems downright lethal.

In one fluid motion, one arm places me on the ground while the other reaches for Johnny's throat and Maverick's meaty fingers grip onto his opponent's windpipe like it's Willy Wonka's last golden ticket.

"No! Stop!" I'm shrieking as I climb Maverick's back.

My arms are clinging to his shoulders as I try to pry the two apart, but neither are budging. Johnny is trying to hold his own, but the poor guy is turning blue, and I don't know how much more he can take.

"You're going to kill him! Stop! Please!" I plead with all I have but nothing gives. I might as well be talking to a wall.

Feeling all hope leave me, I drop to my knees, my arms still trailing above me as I cling to Maverick's legs. This action seems to break my protector from his trance because he's now looking at me, a visible shudder wracking his body while his eyes rake over my bare flesh.

The climbing must have jostled my top and my breasts are now exposed to both men, and what I see shakes me to my core.

Hunger like no other blazes in Maverick's eyes. The man is starved for every inch of me as his jaw clenches and his stare roams me up and down.

I can't help it. The sheer lust running through me has a whimper escaping from my lips and it's enough to break the spell I cast on the man of my dreams. Just like a red flag, the sound turns Maverick into a raging bull and there's no stopping what ensues.

As if on instinct, Maverick's head whips back to Johnny whose stare is locked on me. "Eyes off her, or I'll rip them out."

Johnny laughs sardonically. "Oh, this is rich. You do know she works at a titty bar, right?"

I've never once felt dirty for what I do, but right now, listening to Johnny, I can't help but feel icky. My arms quickly wrap around my body protecting it from unwanted glances and Maverick doesn't miss a beat, with a rapid one-two, he's punched out Johnny's eyes—the bouncer now stumbling back into the door he'd closed not moments before.

"What in-the-ever-loving—" Candy walks in and gasps at the site before her. "Melissa?! You know the rules! No boyfriends in the club! This is grounds for termination." She's rushing over to poor Johnny who's a crumpled mess on the floor while Mav looks like he doesn't have a lick of guilt for the chaos he's just caused.

"Good. She isn't coming back." He's narrowing his eyes at my manager, and I swear he's just signed his death warrant.

"Maverick!" I get up, momentarily forgetting about my state of undress.

But I'm quickly reminded by his laser focus dropping to my chest, his eyes narrowing before he averts his gaze.

"No, I think he's right. You pull in clients, honey, but no talent is worth taking out our best muscle."

At this Mav snorts, smug either about the fact that he just took out what she calls their *best* or that he's gotten me fired.

"Candy, please! Give me another chance. He isn't my boyfriend, and this is just a misunderstanding."

She looks between the three of us, an eyebrow raised. "He isn't your boyfriend?"

"No. Definitely not. He's my brother's best friend. A little overprotective, but not my boyfriend." I look toward Maverick and see that his arms are crossed over his chest, but he doesn't dispute me. *Thank God.* I'd strangle him on the spot if he did.

"Tell you what. Since you *are* a customer favorite, I'll let you take the night off and handle—whatever this is. But I expect you back tomorrow night, and if you give me any more shit, you're out. You hear me?" She's pursing her lips, her arched brow reaching higher if that's even possible.

"Yes, Candy. Thank you so much." I'm practically bowing in gratitude when Maverick places his flannel over me, his thick arms cradling me in that bridal position once more.

"Not your boyfriend my ass," Candy mumbles under her breath as she leans down to assess Johnny's damage.

I'm about to reassure her one last time but I'm carried through the threshold before I can say a word. And as the chilly night air dances across my skin, it dawns on me that this is what I wanted. *But if so, then why does this victory feel so hollow?*

Chapter Three
HUNTER

T<small>HIS GIRL IS GOING TO BE THE DEATH OF ME</small>. *F<small>UCK</small>*. I steal glances as the truck bounces up the steep mountain road, and it's a big mistake.

The truck isn't the only thing jostling and the flannel I threw over her isn't done up, exposing the inner curves of her breasts with every bump in the road.

And I'd be lying if I said if I weren't looking forward to Deadman's pass. That tiny strip is craggier than cottage cheese. It's sure to make the ladies come out and play.

Dammit. That's so fucked up. This is Ericson's little

sister, and she's *barely* turned eighteen and I'm half way to forty.

"So, are you going to tell me what gives? You can't just kidnap me whenever you feel like it." Melissa's tone is pure ice. She isn't even looking my way, and I have to say, it bothers me.

Maybe it's selfish, but I've gotten used to her attention and this new 'I don't give a fuck' attitude is throwing me for a loop. No, I've never acted on her fixation before. *It's wrong. It's sick.*

Which is exactly why I needed to get the hell out of dodge when the thoughts of her started to skew into the forbidden.

"Well?! I'm waiting." She's finally turned to me, her eyes narrowed in disgust. *Another novelty.*

With a deep sigh, I slow the truck, giving her one small glance and apparently it was the wrong thing to do. In her agitation, Melissa has managed to expose herself to me for the second time today and I don't think my cock can take it.

I'm a throbbing mess beneath my zipper, the thick rod pulsing in need. Need of her undoubtedly tight pussy.

"Jesus, Mel. Put those things away." I let my eyes drift back to the road, and just in time as we reach Deadman's Pass.

Melissa releases a little squeak before she's moving her delectable body closer to mine. "He isn't here, Maverick. And what he doesn't know won't hurt him."

Just when I thought my cock couldn't get any harder,

Melissa places a small hand on my lap, her slender fingers trailing up and dangerously close to my throbbing member.

"*Goddammit, Mel!* I told you, no!" With every bit of strength I possess, I rip her hand from my body and instantly regret it.

It feels wrong. Wrong to deny her touch. Wrong to ignore whatever spark this is between us.

And as soon as my eyes land on hers, I know it was wrong because it's hurt her, my baby doll.

Water pools in those azure eyes and I know I've fucked up. Needing to remedy the situation, I go to touch her face, but Mel pulls away. "Don't. Don't touch me."

My head rears back and the truck swerves, I'd taken my eyes off the road for a second too long, lost in the misstep of my actions. As expected, the road takes no mercy on me, and one of the embedded boulders gives way—making us slide off the road and into the ditch leading us straight to certain death.

Everything flashes before me, my life, Melissa, her body and her soul. The last two, precious things I've yet to taste.

Melissa's screams pierce through my mental fog, and the reality that if I don't right us right-the-fuck-now we're as good as dead hits me like a ton of bricks.

There's a small ledge to the left of the ravine, and if I miss it, that's it.

Swerving in that direction, I pray with all that I have for

the truck to hold, hitting the brakes and sliding at just the right angle to keep us alive.

One. Two. Three.

The following seconds drip by slower than molasses, but in the end, I know I must've been good in a past life. The truck comes to a stop with a jerk, our bodies flinging forward, and on instinct my arms reach for Mel.

She'd taken off her seatbelt, making her lithe body fling toward the windshield. Fuck me over and call it my end, but Mel? She still has her whole life ahead of her and I could never forgive myself if anything happened to her because of me.

Bringing her practically naked body to mine, I grip her hard, unable to stop myself from taking in a breath of her peaches and cream scent. God, she smells so good. My dick takes notice too, the fucker jumping up and against her bikini-clad ass, something that makes her startle. Right then, her big blue eyes find mine and there's such vulnerability in them that it threatens to break me on the spot.

"Mav?" She's trembling, the adrenaline of the moment catching up with her.

"Shh, baby doll. You're okay. We're safe." I rip my eyes from her, assessing our precarious position on the ravine's edge. Truth is, we're safe—*for now*. I'm not sure how much longer the ground will hold us.

She's nodding, her hands gripping onto my shirt as she brings herself closer. Closer, but not close enough.

"We need to get out of the truck. See if there's a way to make it back up to the road."

My brave girl nods once more, her face becoming solemn with resolve. "Okay. Let's do it."

Pride fills my chest at her strength, this girl that had been so ready to give up on life not three years ago, yet here she is, not batting a lash.

"Atta girl." I give her ass a little smack before carrying her bridal style, the action causing the prettiest blush to settle over her cheeks, and I'd be lying if I said I didn't like the effect I have on her.

What can I say? I'm one sick fuck.

"On the count of three I'm going to open this door and get us out. No matter what, you hang onto me as if your life depends on it. You hear me, baby?"

"I hear you." Mel gives me a jerky nod, her eyes closing in the process.

"One, Two…" I wrench open the door and jump out with Melissa in my arms, taking a massive breath of fresh air when the ground doesn't give beneath us.

Not wanting to test our luck any further, I make haste up the side of the mountain, using every bit of knowledge I have to avoid soft spots and get us to safety.

In the minutes that seem like hours, I've managed to switch Melissa onto my back, having her climb me like a spider monkey and allowing me the ability to get us to the top faster. Yes, having her in this position made it easier for our climb, but it sure as fuck wasn't easier on my cock.

Her breasts rubbing against my back paired with the heat of her pussy pressed against me had my mind drifting to activities not suited for climbing. It was sheer torture and reaching the top should give me reprieve from these wayward thoughts. *It should.* But it doesn't.

As Melissa's body slides off of my own, I feel every curve and all of the softness that is her, my body instantly becoming addicted to the sensation of her body against mine. *Not good.* This just won't do.

"What now?" Melissa, who has managed to wreck me in every way possible, is looking up at me with such innocence and worry that it takes every bit of lead out of my selfish cock, putting me in check and getting my head on straight.

"We walk until we reach a break in the cliff. It'll let us go deeper into the mountain and camp out for the night until day brakes. It isn't safe out here. The road is too narrow and if anyone were to drive by, I wouldn't trust them to take us out."

Melissa shiver's and I know that if I want to keep her safe, I need to get us settled for the night ASAP.

"Here." I place a hand on her lower back, guiding her off the road and into the woods.

"Do you know where we're going?" Mel peers back at me over her shoulder and I swear I've never seen anything as pretty.

"Of course I do." And that's the truth. This is my terrain. Where I feel the most comfortable. "One of my hunting cabins is up ahead, just north of here. About a twenty-minute hike."

At this she stops, her lithe body colliding against mine and making my cock twitch. *Down boy.*

"Twenty minutes?" She looks down at her feet and it's then I see that she's barefoot.

"What happened to your shoes?"

Melissa rolls her eyes, "I'd kicked them off in the car."

I suck in my lips and nod. There's no way in hell she'll make the walk like this. Without even thinking, I pick her up and throw her over my shoulder, her small hands pressing against my back as I carry her fireman style.

"Maverick! What are you doing!?"

"Protecting your feet." But truth be told, if I carried her the way I did when I was climbing up the mountain, I don't think I'd be able to hold back. One more second of her tits rubbing up against me and I'd be rutting into her like an animal in heat.

"Fine, but your huge shoulder is digging into my stomach." Just then she wiggles her ass, the ass which happens to be right by my head and I don't know if this position is any better. *Fuck me.* This is going to be one long hike.

Chapter Four
MELISSA

Darkness surrounds us as Maverick finally lowers me onto the porch of a small cabin. "This is yours?"

"Yes."

That's it, that's all I get. And as soon as we step inside, I see why. It's an exact replica of the cabin I share with Mila. Down to the placement of the ladder leading up to the tiny loft.

"Um, Maverick?"

He grunts as he reaches for a lantern, lighting it and letting the soft flicker of light fill the room with warmth.

"Why do you have the same tiny house as me?" My

eyes are narrowing on his large frame, but I suspect I know what his answer will be.

"Because I built both with my bare hands. It'd be a waste of energy trying to recreate a new floor plan for each one of my hunting cabins." He's raising a brow as he heads over to the small wood stove, filling it with the stash of firewood to its right.

He's acting like it's no big deal, that he's just admitted to being the owner of my home. The place I've called a safe haven for the past three years.

"Maverick." I'm standing stock-still in the middle of the room, unwilling to move until his eyes are on me.

A beat passes, but once the fire is lit and the room is all aglow, his eyes land on mine and what I see behind them has me stumbling back. Hunger and... *love?*

With a growl, Maverick stands from his crouched position, his heavy steps only stopping once he's right in front of me. "What, Baby Doll?"

"Why didn't you tell me?"

He scoffs. "Do you not remember fifteen-year-old Mel? She would never have agreed to stay if I did."

He's right. I was fiercely independent. Still am. Hell, I wouldn't even agree to stay with my brother. I was on a mission to prove myself. To prove that I didn't need my mother, let alone my father or brother.

As if reading my thoughts, Maverick smirks. "That's what I thought."

Without another word, he picks me up bridal style and

carries me closer to the fire. He's lowering me onto some bedding when the flannel I'd been wearing parts, the thin material giving way to my exposed breasts and making this grown man hiss.

"*Goddammit, Mel.*" He quickly pulls the material closed, his eyes averting toward a dark corner of the room. "Keep those things covered. *Please.*"

He grits that last word out and I can't help but feel a small sense of victory. Even though he claims to not want me, the truth is there in the clenching of his jaw and the twitching of his hand. *Oh, he wants me.* I just need to break him. Show him it's okay to take me.

"We don't have any food here, but I suspect you weren't going to be doing any eating while at the club." He releases a huff of annoyance as he gets up and secures a latch on the door. "I meant it, Mel. I don't want you working there anymore."

"*Maverick.*" It's my turn to be annoyed. "You can't just tell me what to do. Especially since you go disappearing on me, only showing up when you want or need something... and what that is? Who fucking knows!"

I'm frustrated, needing to know what makes this man tick. He follows me around for three goddamn years and then gets to come and go as he pleases? Well, no more. I will not be on bated breath waiting for glimpses of my crush.

"*What do I need?*" He chuckles sardonically before he

repeats it once more, his lips splitting into a maniacal grin. "*What do I need?*"

Before I can stand and really give him a piece of my mind, his large frame is on mine, one of his broad knees kicking open my thighs as he presses it hard against my throbbing core. "Little girl, what I need, I can't fucking have. So it's best you stop asking questions you can't have answers to."

Slay me where I lay. This man is going to be my end.

Why do his words only make me want him more? He's still looming over me, his wide chest heaving up and down to the savage beat of my heart.

Unable to help myself, I grind down on his leg, rolling my hips and rubbing my aching clit against the material of his jeans.

Biting back a whimper, I see the flare in his eyes, the moment where his hunger turns into a fire so bright it threatens to consume us both.

"Fuuuuuck, baby. Don't do that. Don't start something you know we can't finish."

I shiver at his words, my body vibrating beneath his. "We could… if you wanted." Raising a hand, I let my fingernails trail down the thin material of his shirt, enjoying every ridge and dip of his hard chest and toned abs. "I could be all yours."

Maverick closes his eyes, an involuntary shudder wracking his body. "God, I bet you have such a pretty pussy." He presses his knee harder against me and I lose all air. "So soft and pink. And just for me. *Just for Daddy.*"

Surprise registers on both of our faces but it's quickly wiped away by the hunger that rages deep within us. His words have unlocked a hidden desire, a secret thirst that only he can quench. And it's his words alone that have the power to make me come, but I refuse to get there alone. Letting my hand trail lower, I press it against an impressive bulge, so impressive it gives me pause. *Will it even fit?*

It doesn't matter because Maverick is ripping my hand from his body. "Fuck, Mel. I said we can't."

He's standing faster than I have time to process what's just happened. All I know is that his rejection stings more than I thought possible and that my vision is quickly clouding. Especially after that moment we've just shared.

Doing the only thing I know how; I turn my back to the room and shut down. A self-preservation technique I thought I'd mastered until now.

"Fine. We can't, but I bet someone at the club could." I'm so full of shit. I would never sleep with one of those guys, but right now I'm hurting, and there's no stopping the verbal diarrhea that's coming out of my mouth. "Hell, maybe it'll even be Johnny."

"You little brat." Before the tears have a chance to fall, I'm being wrenched onto my back, a massive bulge being pressed against my core. "You open those legs for no one, you hear?"

He thrusts into my bikini-clad slit, and I swear I see stars.

"I can't hear you, Mel. Say it." Another thrust and I'm wrapping my legs around his thick torso like my life depends on it. And right now, it does. I need to chase this release like I need air. "Tell me you'll keep those legs closed, like a good little girl."

"*Oh, fuck.* So good." I'm lost in my head, rubbing against him, rolling my aching clit and seeking more friction. "You feel so—"

But I don't finish my sentence because large hands come to either hip, stopping my movement and in turn stopping my release.

"No, baby. You can't come until you promise me. These legs stay closed, do you hear?" He's growling down at me, but I refuse to give in that easily.

"No, *Daddy*." Using a self-defense move Eric taught me, I maneuver out from underneath Maverick's large frame, only stopping once I've come to a standing position to his right.

"How will I dance for anyone if I can't open my legs…" I let the flannel fall from my body, the act leaving me in nothing more than my panties. "And how will I dance, if I can't do this…"

Lifting one leg at a time, I straddle the now seated man, lowering just enough so that my heat is right above his swollen bulge. Unable to stop myself, I press down on it, stroking the thick shaft up and down with my heated flesh.

God, this feels so good. I hope he doesn't make me stop. *Oh, he won't.* With one look into his amber-colored eyes, I know this man is as good as mine.

Hunter

"Fuck, baby. You better not be doing this for anyone else." My eyes lock on where our bodies connect and I can't help but dig my calloused fingers deep into her hips, the motion helping her rub me up and down.

It's slow and methodical, pulling us both into a trance. Up. Down. Just a little more. A little more and I know I'll get her there, where she needs to be. "Promise me, baby. Promise Daddy and I'll let you cream all over my aching cock."

"Yes, God. Please… *I promise.*" Her hands clamp on to either side of my shoulders, her movements now frantic as she chases her release. "Give it to me. Please."

Christ, I'm one sick motherfucker. It should be illegal, the way my dick throbs from hearing this girl beg for me. It's wrong. So fucking wrong.

Mel is too young, too pure for the shit I want to do to her. Yet here I am, not giving a fuck that her brother would have a coronary if he knew I was letting her get off on my hard length.

"Fuck it. I'm already going to hell."

Decision made, I shove her back, just enough to give

myself enough space. And ever so slowly, I undo my zipper, knowing that there's no coming back from what I'm about to do.

With a groan, I pull out my hard length and give it a hard tug, the fucker jerking in protest, and I swear it knows I'm not letting it inside that tight little cunt.

Down boy. You're just here for her.

"Come here, baby, and ride Daddy's cock like a goddamn Slip 'N Slide." With both hands on her plush hips, I pull her lace covered slit closer, nestling her lips atop my thick ridge.

Fuuuuuck, that feels good. Too good. Lord help me, I wasn't planning on sliding inside her warm heat, but I'm not sure how much of this I can take.

"Oh, Daddy. It's perfect. Fucking perfect. Thick and straight, fat and pink." She grinds on my length as she makes a desperate keening sound, and I swear I see stars.

With her next upward thrust, my back tightens and balls draw up with need—the need to shove myself so deep inside her, it fills her up with the promise of a future. *A future we could never have.*

Just then, Mel digs her nails into my shoulders and a full-bodied shudder takes over her tiny frame. *Exquisite.* That's what she is.

"That's right, baby. Take your pleasure. Rub that little pussy. Get it nice and sopping wet for me."

Mel whines as her bottom lip pushes out in a pout. "More. I need more. Please. I need it inside."

God, how could I deny her?

I can't. I won't. I need her just as bad as she needs me.

With calloused fingers, I take hold of my girth, stroking it from base to tip—*once, twice*—before I'm nudging her lace panties to the side and teasing the drenched slit, up and down.

There she is, that tight little bundle of nerves. As soon as I glide against it, my baby shudders, her little pussy clenching against my swollen head.

"So responsive. What do you think? Is she ready for Daddy's cock?"

Mel is shaking against me, her legs squeezing against my thighs as she nods. "Yes. Ready. So ready."

That's it. That does it. I need no more prompting. "Take it, baby. Take all of it. Every. Fucking. Inch."

And with one swift thrust, I'm shoving my hard length deep inside her, the pain and pleasure instantly notifying me of what I've just done. Holy shit. She's fucking tight. Virgin tight. "*Fucking hell, baby!*"

Mel whimpers, the pain riddled across her face further indication that I've just taken something I had no right to.

"*Goddammit!*" I roar into the room, my vocal cords vibrating against the column of my throat. I need to see it. The proof of what will forever be mine.

Mel's face contorts as I slowly pull her up off my shaft, the tinge of pink telling of the secret she no longer holds.

"*Baby doll.*" It's but a whisper, the sight threatening to take my breath away. This just confirms it, she's mine.

Bringing her body back down, I impale her on me once more. "You've gone and done it now. My naughty girl." Dropping one of my hands, I rear it before bringing it down hard against her ass with a slap. "You're going to pay for that. Tricking me into fucking that virgin pussy."

I'm bouncing her up and down on my lap now, both of my hands around her waist as I lift her up and down like a fuck toy.

"If you think I'm going to take it easy on that sweet cunt, you're mistaken."

And with my next thrusts, she answers in only the way she can. "Sorry, Daddy!"

Right then, I press the pad of my thumb to her tiny pearl, rubbing it and making her eyes roll back in her head, pleasure completely taking over her features.

"That's right, baby. Bounce on that fat cock." With a free hand, I grab hold of her face, squeezing her jaw and bringing our lips together in a kiss that is nothing short of possessive. I'm conveying all that I feel, all that I am and all she is. We are one. At this moment, we are all there is.

"Too much. So much. So good." Mel cries into my mouth.

"I'm glad you like it, baby doll, because I've got no plans of slowing down." Just then, I trail a hand up her throat and back to her nape, letting my fingers delve into the thickness of her hair before I'm yanking her away from my lips.

"*Mmmmm*. This pussy, baby." I yank her head back

even further, the action exposing the column of her neck and allowing my tongue to trail up the tender flesh. "It's mine. All fucking mine. I own it. I'm marking it."

Yes, my words may have her walls contracting around me, but it's her next words that have me shooting a rogue spurt into her womb. "Yes, Daddy, please. Mark me. Make me yours."

"Jesus, you're going to make me spill." I wrap one hand around her waist while the other moves to one of her juicy tits. "God help me, these tits." Deft fingers massage the sensitive mound before I'm slapping at its side and making it jiggle just right. "Fuck, you're perfect. Every inch of you. My perfect baby."

My praise seems to be her undoing because, one more thrust and I watch her come apart, unfolding like the prettiest of flowers as she shouts her release.

And lord, if that wasn't enough, this girl squeezes my cock, milking it with every shake and shudder she gives.

I'm about to blow, but because I'm one greedy bastard, I want more and I'm taking more.

Dragging a hand down her back, I seek out that tight little hole, not stopping until I'm pressing a finger against the small ring of muscles.

She's still riding out her release when I press just the tip inside, the action taking her by surprise but making her moan even louder. "Such a good girl, letting Daddy fill all her pretty holes."

Holyfuckingshit. Mel contracts around me like never

before, her already tight pussy squeezing the soul right out of my body. I see nothing but black as wave after wave of pleasure washes over me. *Heaven.* This must be it.

There's no holding back, rope after sticky rope of cum spills inside her. The sensation of my warm release coating her and dripping down her walls making us both shudder with even more pleasure. *How's this even possible? How is such joy allowed?*

I have no fucking clue. All I know is that I'm a thief and that this moment was stolen. Stolen from a girl whose innocence did not belong to me.

For three goddamn years, I trailed her, making sure to keep her safe. But tonight? Tonight, I failed.

That's something I should never live down, and I have no intention of doing so.

Chapter Five
MELISSA

A SOFT RUSTLING WAKES ME FROM THE DEEPEST SLEEP. I don't think I've had a good night's rest like this since I was a child. And just like a vivid dream, memories of last night flood me, heating my body and making me hungry for more. *Where is my mountain man?*

We must've fallen asleep next to the wood stove, because the last thing I remember is closing my eyes to the sensation of bliss. Turning back toward the room, I see Maverick. He's at the door and his face is as stoic as ever.

"Good morning, handsome." I stretch, letting my eyes fully drink in his massive frame.

"We need to get going." His tone is harsh, his words rushed. *What the fuck.*

"Maverick?" There's a crack in my voice, I can't hide it. His complete one-eighty has my chest squeezing.

"Melissa." He stares at me blankly as if we didn't just spend the most amazing night together. "We need to go."

"Oh, we're not going anywhere until you tell me what the hell is going on here." I stand to my full five-foot-six, and walk toward him, only stopping once I'm a hair's breadth away. "You don't get to follow me around for three years, kidnap me from my job, and then bounce me on your cock like your little plaything, only to turn around and act like all of that was just in my head." My head is craned all the way back, glaring at this motherfucker who thinks he can just blow off whatever this is. "Well? I'm waiting for an answer."

Maverick closes his eyes, his head softly shaking left to right as his large hands go to his hips. "I'm sorry, Mel. It's my fault. All of it."

I'm taken aback by his words. Definitely not what I was expecting. My brows drop as they push together. "*What*? What do you mean?"

"I should've never started trailing you in the first place. That was something your father should've done."

I scoff, the idea of that man doing anything other than worrying about where his next bottle of booze was coming from sounds absolutely ridiculous to me.

"I don't need a father. And last night you made it pretty

clear that you wanted to be my Daddy." I step closer, shoving a finger into his hard chest. "And the way I see it? A Daddy is way better than a drunk-ass father."

A shudder wracks his frame, but I don't think it's one of pleasure. "Baby doll, that's just it. You're too pure for shit like this. Hell, you were a virgin up until last night and I ruined that. I ruined that for you, and you'll never get it back." He turns away from me, his frame facing the door now. "The least I could do is let you go. Live a life without me tarnishing it further. No, I should've been pushing you closer to your brother. Kicked your dad's ass and made him act right, for your sake."

I'm outright laughing now, tears streaming down my face and I'm not sure if they're from Maverick's rejection or the absurdity of this all. "An ass-whooping wouldn't have fixed that man, and Eric is just that, my brother. I'm not looking for a father. I don't need that. I've already done and raised myself. What I want is a man. But apparently, that's not you." Now it's my turn to shake my head. "I will not chase you. You either want me or you don't."

A beat passes and there's nothing but silence that eats the distance between us. *Fuck this.* Fuck this awkward moment and fuck this bullshit man.

I've come too far in life, battling the rejection of a mother and then father, only to let this shit trip me up again. *Never again. Never again will I fight for someone to see my worth.*

Without looking back, I storm out of the cabin, not

giving a damn that I'm barefoot. My feet could be bloody stumps of meat before I'd let this man ever touch me again.

A BED. A COMFY-COZY BED. THAT'S ALL I WANT RIGHT now. It's been nothing but deafening silence with Jekyll and Hyde, and that's just fine with me. I just want to get home, to my little cabin and crawl into deep sleep. Shove the memories of the past twenty-four hours deep in a hole where I won't have to relive them over and over.

Just as the feel of his body entering mine is about to start looping in my head. I see it. A break in the woods up ahead. *The road!*

With a few more steps I'm on the pavement, broody man in tow. *Finally.* Now how long before we get back into town.

And as if by divine intervention, it isn't long. Just then, a loud booming voice comes over a speaker. "Everyone okay?"

It's Eric, my brother!

Never have I been so happy to see a park ranger, and I'm about to run toward him in gratitude when I finally register the expression on his face. He's getting out of the truck when his eyes flicker back between Maverick and me. His features speaking of nothing but violence and it's all being directed at the man who's saved my life on more than one occasion.

Taking action, I step between them, ready to take Eric's heat.

"Talk. Now." My brother's eyes are trained on the man behind me, completely ignoring my presence.

"Eric Ericson! Don't talk to him like that!" I shove him, but his body barely moves, save for his brows which are pushing together. I may be mad at Maverick, but I still owe him my life.

"Mel? What the fuck are you wearing?" He goes to move the flannel, but Maverick pulls me back into his body, his arms wrapping possessively around my torso.

"I wouldn't do that if I were you, brother."

Shit. He's right. I'm naked underneath and that would've been a show I'm sure Eric would've liked to have missed, even though he's not acting like it at the moment.

My brother scoffs. *"Excuse me?"*

I suck in a lungful of air, gathering courage. "He's saving your eyes and your mind from an inevitable bleach bath, bro. I'm talking BlackBerry-BleachBit annihilation."

Eric is looking down at me, his eyes blinking before they're flashing back to Maverick and if looks could kill, there'd be nothing but a pile of ash behind me.

"Step aside, Mel." My brother goes to move me, but Maverick only presses me harder into his chest.

"She isn't moving, Ericson." I don't know what's going on, but I swear I feel Maverick vibrating behind me. "We fell over a hundred feet down that ravine and there's no way in hell I'm letting her out of my sight until a doctor has cleared her."

At this, Eric balks, his head swiveling around and taking inventory of the missing truck and the skid chunk of road missing up ahead. "Answer me this. How in the fuck did driving off Deadman's Pass lead to my sister being buck naked?"

Eric's jaw ticks as he waits for Maverick's response, and I think this is where he's going to let my secret out. Yeah, it's well-known that my brother and me aren't the closest, but he would still lose his shit if he found out where I was working.

A beat passes, and then another, the time only angering Eric more. "Well, are you going to fucking answer me or what?"

"It's not my business to tell, brother."

"Oh, don't you brother me with this bullshit. You're dead to me. I'm not sure how you made it out of that fall alive, and for that I'm grateful, at least for my sister's sake. But you? You're fucking dead." Eric grabs my wrist and yanks, the action hurting so bad it makes me wince.

"Drop your hand or lose it." Maverick growls from behind and the look that crosses my brother's face is something between shock and confusion. "She's clearly hurt, and you're only making it worse."

Eric blinks rapidly before the shock fades and anger takes its place. "I can see that. That's why she's coming with me. I have a truck and she obviously needs to get to a doctor." My brother paces in front of us, both hands in his hair as his face contorts in disgust. "Look, I don't know how long this has been going on between you two, but Melissa just turned eighteen. I can't in good conscience leave her here with you."

"Whoa, whoa, whoa. This is not what it looks like. I don't see your sister that way." Maverick says this with such vehemence that my body instinctively recoils, needing to get away from the man that's hurt me with his words.

If he doesn't see me that way, then what was last night? Was it all a game?

Pulling myself from Maverick's hold, I take a few steps closer to my brother, reaching out and placing a soothing hand on his back.

"He's right, Eric. Maverick doesn't want me." And with those words I turn to look at the man who's owned my heart for the better part of two years. The man who apparently can't even stand to look at me right now.

"She's right. She is and forever will be your little sister." Maverick's eyes are trained on my brother's truck, his jaw clenching as he gives one jerky nod. "And you're right. She needs to get to a doctor and you're the only one who can get her there."

"Finally, some fucking reason." Ericson goes to grab me but Maverick steps forward with lightning speed, sweeping me off the ground and placing me protectively in his arms.

"But you're not manhandling her." Maverick doesn't

even look back while he says this, completely missing my brother's bewildered expression as he trails behind us and rounds the car.

"Fine. I'm letting you come with us to see the doc, but as soon as we arrive, you'd better disappear. I'm not above calling the Sheriff."

"Eric!" I shriek as Maverick lowers me into the cab of the truck.

"What? This..." he waves between Maverick and me, "This shit isn't normal, Mel. I'm no fool. It didn't just happen."

Maverick is sliding in beside me, his thumb and forefinger pinching at the bridge of his nose. "Just get us to the doc, Ericson. We'll talk later."

"Oh, there'll be no talking. I have nothing more to say to you." My brother huffs as the truck's engine rumbles on. "You're dead to me. Fucking dead."

Chapter Six
MELISSA

"So, he just disappeared?" Mila looks over at me from the tiny kitchenette like I've just told her the Pope was a lizard person. "But that doesn't make any sense. That man has been your shadow for the past three years. He can't just go missing like this."

"He didn't go missing. My brother pushed him away and he gladly went." I let out a long sigh as I examine the newly acquired cast on my arm. "It's never been clearer that Maverick only saw me as an obligation. As soon as I turned eighteen, he disappeared. First on that three-month hiatus right when I started working at The Pearl and now this."

It's been forty-eight hours since I've seen my broody crush, and truth be told, the ache I feel inside is slowly killing me. The moments we shared deep in those woods will live with me forever. I guess the same can't be said for him.

"Hey, I need a change of topic ASAP, or I'm bound to disintegrate into a puddle of tears." My eyes round as I pout at my friend. I've yet to tell her about what went down in the cabin, and I'm not about to do so now. *I'm not ready.* "Please, pleeeeease. Let's talk about something less depressing."

"Fine. I'm going to Florida." Mila looks at me as if she's just told me she's going down to the store, not clear cut across the country.

"What?!" I sit up from the tiny loveseat and stare her down. "When were you planning on telling me?!"

She lets out a small chuckle. "Chill, girl. I just found out a couple of days ago. Catherine is pregnant and needs my help with her business. Says she's having really bad morning sickness and could use the extra hand."

My head rears back as my brows furrow. "But that woman never wanted you in the same room as her work stuff, let alone touching it." And it's true. Mila's mom is a raging bitch if I've ever seen one. "I don't know this just doesn't seem right. You sure she's not trying to lure you down there so she can swipe one of your kidneys. You are her mini me after all. Maybe she's just wanting to use you for spare parts."

Mila sucks in a breath and flings a hand to her chest. "Mel! That's fucking horrible! Have you been listening to my true crime podcasts without me?"

I snort. "That does sound like something they'd cover. But nah. I'm still stuck on my Jessa Kane binge."

My best friend shakes her head and chuckles. "You and that daddy kink of yours."

"Hey, don't knock it until you've read it." *Or lived it.* But I don't say that last part. Raising a brow, I grill her for details. "So tell me, when are you leaving?"

"Tomorrow morning."

My brows practically hit my hairline. "What?!"

"Yeah. I just wanted to make sure you'd be okay without me." Her lips push to the side in an awkward smile and my chest warms.

Neither of us may have doting mothers, but we have each other and that's a lot. "Girl, you didn't have to wait on me. But I appreciate it and you." I get up from my position on the loveseat and walk the few steps toward the kitchenette where Mila had been standing, my arms wrapping around her as soon as I've reached her. "Seriously, girl. Love you to pieces, but your ass didn't have to wait around on me."

My best friend snorts. "You're like my sister, Mel. No way in hell I was leaving you until I knew you'd be okay."

At this I pull back, my brows furrowing. "It's just a fracture, Mila."

Mila shakes her head. "No, I'm talking about Maverick. I heard how he came into the Pearl and how he knocked the ever-living-shit out of Johnny." She winces before looking away. "And with how mopey you've been lately, I just wanted to make sure you were going to be okay."

I laugh on a sigh. "Mopey? I didn't think I was that bad."

"Girl, your spirit animal could be that sad looking bunny. You know, the Vizcacha? It always looks so depressed and like it's ready to take a nap."

I snort and shake my head. That sounds about right, but I'm not copping to it.

"Nah, I'll be fine, girl. You just worry about yourself. Seems to me like you'll be dealing with the Wicked Witch, but on heightened hormones. You sure you don't want me to come with you as backup?"

Mila grins at me while shaking her head no. "Not right now, but I just might."

"Alright. Let's go get you packed. You know I'm always a speed-dial away." And with that, I swat her ass with my good hand and head up to the tiny loft we share. This space might be small, but it'll sure feel enormous once she's gone.

Truth be told, she's been my lifeline all these years and this'll be the longest we've been apart. But as we ascend the narrow ladder, I tell myself it'll be okay, because I'm one bad bitch and I'm not about to let any man get me down. Not even *Him*.

Two weeks later...

Blonde strands of hair whip against my face to AC/DC's Highway to Hell as I speed down a small dirt road. I've got the windows down and the sun is shining bright, instantly improving my mood.

Never have I felt so free as I do now, a new sense of empowerment running through me as I realize I've made it a whole twenty-four hours without aching for a man that'll never see me as anything more than his best friend's little sister.

And yes, I'm thinking about him now. But I hadn't been —*for a whole day*—and that's a step forward. The man doesn't want me.

That was made painfully obvious when he bailed on me for the second time. I'm not sure where he's disappeared to, or why, but a man doesn't have to tell me twice that he doesn't want me. And if the look of indifference on his face as we got to the hospital wasn't enough, then his radio silence these past two weeks has been.

Sure, he's made the rare appearance at the club—thankfully, avoiding Johnny when he does—but he's always gone by the time my shift ends, and I swear, he barely spares me a glance while he's there.

Whatever. My cast is finally off, and I'm going to see Mila. It's a good day. I'm having a good day.

"You've arrived." A disembodied voice comes over the speakers, cutting into the song and into my sad little pep-talk.

Looking out about half a mile down the road, I see it. The large white farmhouse on the hill. *It's stunning.* I can't believe this is what Mila's been hiding.

A lot has happened over the past couple of weeks. For starters, Mila found herself a Daddy.

Sure, it's one hell of a taboo situation since, technically, he got her mom pregnant first. But love is love right? Who's to let a botched one-night-stand get in the way of their happily ever after?

And to our surprise, his family's ranch had been just over the mountain this entire time. So naturally, when said Daddy called me for an impromptu surprise birthday for Mila, I agreed.

Yes, we'd already celebrated before she'd left for Florida, but I was in a pitiful state. And as much as I love our birthday traditions, I couldn't say no to meeting the man that's had my girl in knots for the first time in her life.

Mila Kournikova doesn't date—*hell, she doesn't even flirt*—so this Crown guy must be something special. There's nothing that could keep me away. Not even depressing thoughts of Maverick.

The beat-up Civic Mila and I share comes to a stop and I'm able to fully take in the massive wrap-around porch with white rocking chairs and all. It's picture perfect. The stuff happily ever afters are made of, complete with the older lady coming out of the front door. She's dressed right out of the eighteen-hundreds with her long-sleeved blouse, full skirt and apron.

As I step out of my car, I can't help but ask, "Aren't you hot? I'd be sweatin' like a whore in church in that."

The matronly woman chuckles. "You must be Melissa. Jace told us you'd be arriving this afternoon. Mila is at her cabin right now, but they should be here shortly."

"Oh, no worries. I need to go to the ladies' room if possible." I lift my iced coffee in the air and wave it in her direction. "I didn't know how long the drive would take me at first and I drank one too many of these."

The lady chuckles. "Right this way, darling. Coffee just so happens to be my obsession. But it gives me the runs something fierce." I'm cackling as she ushers me up the wooden steps and through the door. "I'm Mary, by the way. But you can call me Nana or Nana Mary."

There's a twinkle in her eye as she says this, and I can't help but feel like I'm missing out on some hidden context. Either way, I've been short on motherly figures all my life, so when one as wholesome and hilarious as this one presents itself, I'm not letting it go.

"Alright, Nana Mary. Point me toward the restroom."

Wow. This place is massive. I'm taking a turn out of the bathroom when I forget where I came from. There are so many hallways, I'm not sure where to go.

"You lost there, princess?" A deep voice calls from behind me and I startle, dropping what's left of my iced coffee on what looks to be an antique runner.

"Shit!" I'm cursing under my breath but that only serves to make my shadow laugh.

"I'm sorry about that. Didn't mean to scare you."

The man crouches down next to me, helping me scoop up the melted ice as I hopelessly dab at the rug with the damp napkin that'd been stuck to my cup.

"What a nightmare," I'm mumbling under my breath as I get the last of the ice into the damn cup.

Just then, two fingers press to the underside of my chin, effectively lifting my gaze and what I see blows me away.

Those eyes. I've seen those eyes before. I'm so surprised that I shut my own, unwilling to feel the emotions they evoke.

"Hey, there. It's okay. I promise. It's just an old rug." His voice is completely different from Maverick's, but it's soothing all the same. There's something about the deep tambour that calms me.

"Just an old rug," I scoff, finally opening my eyes and meeting the handsome stranger's. "That's the point. It seems valuable. Precious even."

At this he grins. "It's just a rug. Material things are just that. Material. But a smile like yours? Priceless."

His words have me blinking back tears, fighting the demons in my head, playing a continuous loop of the words I've tried so hard to overcome.

'Worthless bitch. You just fuck everything up, don't you?'

Out of nowhere, someone else cuts into the moment. "Quit trying to bag Mila's bestie, Matthew."

I snort, looking for the voice and see a very pregnant brunette walking next to a petite blonde. "Hi, I'm Penelope and this is Anaya. We're the Crown ladies."

My brows furrow and this amuses the man she called Matthew.

"Oh, this is priceless. She doesn't know about the infamous Crown women, does she?"

I'm even more confused now. "Am I supposed to?"

"See, Mary told us we'd like her." The brunette grabs my arm and links it with hers while the blonde just shakes her head and smiles. "Don't you worry about that stain. Mattie will get it, right? It's the least you can do after trying to put the moves on company." Penelope hollers back at Matthew who's now rolling his eyes.

"Yeah, fine. But tell Jack to move her car. It's not going to be a surprise for Mila if they drive up and see the Civic."

"That's right!" The blonde chimes in, her voice like a delicate tinkle. "The men are in the study. That way you'll get to meet the other brothers. Well, Austin and Jack. I don't know about the lone wolf, he'd spend his life deep in the woods if we'd let him."

"Oh, he'll show up. He wouldn't miss Mary's cooking." Penelope playfully shoves at me as if I were in on the inside joke, making me feel at ease with them both.

"Here we are." Anaya opens a massive wooden door and the scent of tobacco and whiskey hits me, the smell instantly transporting me back to the man that's invaded my heart and soul for so long. *Why is he everywhere?* It's as if I can't escape him. No matter where I go or what I do. *He's everywhere.*

Chapter Seven
HUNTER

Fuck. No matter how hard I try to forget her, I just can't. There's a big part of me that thinks I'm a fucking idiot for agreeing to leave her alone.

But hell, it's Ericson. My best friend of twenty years. The man who's saved me from myself more times than I can count.

His words keep looping in my head, a replay of the last night I saw her continuously flashing in my head.

"There. She's with the doc now." Ericson pushes a finger into my chest. "You can leave."

"Brother, I know what's going through your head, but it isn't like that."

Ericson scoffs. "Brother? Oh, this is something. You're no brother to me. What you've done with my sister, the way she pines for you... it all makes sense now."

He takes a step back, his hands flying to his hair as a look of disgust takes over his features.

"Whoa, I told you, it isn't like that."

Another snort. "You think I'm stupid? The way you were holding her the entire ride here, that shit isn't platonic. You love her."

Now it's my turn to stumble back, my brows pushing together as I fully take in his words. I'm shaking my head, processing the feelings running through me when Ericson continues his assault.

"Don't even bother denying it. And the sick part is that she's barely legal, man. How long have you been after her? Twisting her into your little puppy, hanging on your every word?"

"Hold up now. You can talk all the shit you want about me, but don't you dare fucking talk about her like that." I take two steps forward, shoving my long-time friend against the wall, but he simply laughs in my face.

"And there it is. The damned truth. You love her so damn much that you can't even stand me placing her in a bad light." He gets in my face then. "So, tell me, you sick fuck. How long? How long have you been fucking my little sister behind my back?"

I'm so stunned I just stand there, unmoving until his next set of words have me reacting on instinct.

"Dad was right. She really is just like her momma." With a final shove, Ericson spits out, "How long has that little whore been opening her legs?"

With every bit of fire in my soul, I rear back and punch the living shit out of my friend. Fuck the years, fuck the friendship. I will not have him talking about Mel that way.

And as Ericson crumples to the ground and the shuffling of the security guard's feet come my way, I know I will never regret my time protecting Mel or upholding her honor.

"Sir, I'm calling the Sheriff." *The young man wearing a uniform two sizes too big informs me as he feebly attempts to grab me by the wrists.*

"You go ahead and do that, Barney Fife. I'm not going anywhere."

"Motherfucker." *My old friend grumbles, coming to.* "Stay away from her. I mean it."

Looking down at Ericson's crumpled form, I spit out the words that I'd grow to regret. "You have my word, asshole. I'll stay away from your sister. Not because you asked me to, but because she deserves far better."

Far better than a pervert like me. The dark shit I'm into, it has no place touching something as pure as Mel.

Right then, A slew of nurses shuffle past me, kneeling down to tend to the man I once called brother and a pang of guilt hits me. Yes, he deserved a punch to the head for that comment, but he wasn't wrong when he called me a sick fuck.

And he wasn't. The entire situation was wrong. *So wrong.*

I should've never laid a finger on Mel. But fuck, did it feel good when I did. A little too good.

One night wasn't enough, and the things I'd been imagining with her? Yeah, they were anything but innocent. And that's just it. She's just a girl. Barely turned eighteen.

But even as I say this, I know it's not the whole truth. She might be young, but the things Mel has seen and done... Hell, she's more grown than all the women I've fucked combined.

A sputtering sound breaks me from my thoughts as my Polaris hits gravel on the main drive. *Damn, am I looking forward to tonight's dinner.* Mary's cooking is phenomenal and focusing on my brothers instead of my sad-as-fuck situation should help me get Mel off my mind.

And just as I step off the four-wheeler, I catch a whiff of that peaches and cream scent, wondering if I've finally gone and lost my mind. Even the ghost of this girl is trailing me.

With heavy steps I make my way up the wrap-around porch and thankfully catch a different scent. Buttercream frosting. *Cake.* My second weakness.

Needing a hit of Mary's sweet confections, I practically run toward the kitchen. But I've just reached the threshold when a flash of blonde catches my eye, the sight before me freezing me on impact.

There she is. The woman I've been trying so desperately to avoid. All wrapped up and presented to me as an offering in that tight little dress that hugs her curves like the sweetest of sins.

I'd been in a trance, but Melissa flinging herself at my brother has me snapping the fuck out.

"Come here, big guy. We're practically family, aren't we?" She wraps both arms around his torso and I can't help it. A deep rumble emanates from my chest, my eyes forming into tiny slits as I wish death upon my brother.

A strangled sound comes from the right and I faintly hear my moniker, but my eyes are trained on the tall blonde who's back has gone ramrod straight. *That's right sweetheart, Daddy's here, and he isn't pleased.*

What the fuck?! There it is again. Yes, I've been into play, but never have I delved into Daddy kink—not until her. I thought maybe it was a fluke up at the cabin, but this just proves there's something more. Something this girl stirs inside of me. An urgent need to protect and dominate.

Shit. This is bad. Really bad.

Bright blue eyes turn toward me, and I know I'm fucked. This woman has the power to bring me to my knees. Who was I kidding, thinking I could stay away? Just the thought of it now, of never seeing her again, has me hyperventilating, my chest rising and falling rapidly in sync with my panic.

Something akin to fear and sadness dance in her magical orbs and I feel the urgent need to console her. On instinct, the words I've spoken many times in my head tumble out before I'm able to stop them. "*Baby doll.*"

As soon as I've said it, all emotion vacates her pretty face, and a steeled one of indifference takes over.

"Brother. Everything okay?" A hand clamps down on my shoulder and I see Jace had walked over at some point.

All I can manage is a sharp nod as I assess the room, taking everyone else in. But like a damned magnet, my eyes fling back toward my girl. *My girl.* She isn't really mine and the thought angers me beyond rational thought.

"What is *she* doing here?" I ask my brother while my eyes bore into the woman I could never have.

But it's the little spitfire who answers instead. "I was invited, thank-you-very-much." She places both hands on her hips, hitching up one side, and visions of me taking her over the knee flood my mind—spanking the sass right out of her tight little ass.

Fuck. This is bad. I can't be around her. All this time apart has only served to intensify my need for her. Her body and her soul. I need it like I need my next breath.

She can't be here. Not if I'm going to keep my word to her brother. *Not that he deserves it.*

And if she was invited, then she needs to be un-invited, STAT. "By whom?"

Melissa steps forward, coming toe-to-toe with my looming frame and a shudder wracks me as more images of my body dominating hers flood me. She may be taller than average, but she's still tiny compared to my six-three.

"Mila's stepdaddy invited me." She's glaring at me as she says this, but her words only serve to confuse me. *What the fuck?*

"I'm not her stepfather," and "He's not my stepfather," are uttered simultaneously by Jace and Mel's roommate, the realization of who she's talking about hitting me like a ton of bricks.

Wow. Just wow. Here I've been playing hot potato with Mel while my brother robs the cradle with my girl's roommate. *How had I missed this?*

I've been trailing Melissa for almost three years, and not once did I see my brother cross the girls' paths.

That's when I see her, Catherine, reaching for my girl and pulling her into a forced embrace.

"Melissa. Such a pleasure to see you, dear. You're like crabgrass, aren't you? Always popping up everywhere."

The-fuck?

I'm about to say something when Mel responds, "Did you just compare me to a fucking weed?"

The wretched woman doesn't answer, so I press her for one. "*Did you?*"

Catherine bristles, her face getting all splotchy. "Mila, please explain to your friend that I was just making a statement. There's no need for everyone to get up in arms about it."

Mel's roommate pipes up in annoyance. "She's standing right in front of you, *Mom*. You can tell her yourself."

At that, you'd think the wicked witch would say something, but she remains silent. Yes, I'm well aware of what the girls call her, and with good reason. Catherine is vile. Pure fucking garbage, and I'll be damned if I let her talk down to Melissa like this.

"Apologize. Now," I growl, making Catherine's face turn even redder before she's turning toward my brother.

"Jason?" *Jason?* Yes, that's his birth name, but nobody calls him that. He hates it. Damn, it seems like I've missed a lot.

"What? I believe you did liken Melissa to a weed." Turning toward my brother—who's apparently the holder of many secrets—I see he's fighting back a grin. "Look, it's clear my brother feels offended on this young lady's behalf. The sooner you clarify you meant no ill will, the sooner we can go back to the birthday festivities."

Needing clarity, I ask, "So *you* invited her?"

Jace simply nods, as if it's no big deal. "She's Mila's roommate."

"I know." My eyes fall on Mila Kournikova, a girl with a twisted past and secrets darker than the inkiest black.

"You two know each other?" Catherine asks as she looks back and forth between her daughter and me.

I grunt, if this bitch only knew. "Yes. Now apologize to Melissa."

But instead of an apology, I get Jace's attitude instead.

"Hey. Watch your tone." He nudges me. "Let's keep things light, for Mila's sake. We don't want a brawl ruining her surprise dinner, do we?"

So this is the reason for the get together. I was so lost in my self-pity that I didn't ask for details when Mary called me down.

Just then, the stand-in matriarch of the family mumbles under her breath. "Wouldn't be the first time."

Catherine's eyes go wide at that, and she's quickly turning to my girl. "I meant nothing by it, Mel."

"Mhm." Melissa makes a non-committal sound but drops it.

It's not enough. That apology was half-assed, but out of respect for my brother and his woman, I'll bite my tongue... for now.

"Good. Now that it's handled, how about we make our way into the dining room. Dinner is ready!" Just then, Mary steps in front of me while carrying a huge dish into the fully decked out dining room. *Wow, my brother has it bad.*

And as we all shuffle behind Mary, I can't help but realize that I do too. I'm lost. Lost to a girl who can't be mine, but with every second that passes, I doubt if that'll hold true.

Chapter Eight
MELISSA

Keep it together, girl. Keep. It. Together.

How I've managed to maintain my cool while Maverick is but two feet away, I have no freaking clue. Neither does Mila based on the glances she's throwing me. Yeah, girl. I don't know. Call it my new superpower.

Face of indifference, activate.

It's helpful that the ranch is absolutely breathtaking, this dining room being no exception.

I look around and take a seat at the massive table, taking notice of the intricate molding on the walls and ceilings that speak of a history I'm desperate to discover. That and the decorations for Mila's birthday party has my body humming with a warm sense of joy.

It's clear this family loves each other, and they poured that effort into showing my bestie a good time.

Hey, my life may be a shit show, but at least my best friend's is on the up-and-up. "This is amazing, Mila! *Yes.* It definitely beats our birthday tradition of takeout and T.V."

She sniffles, a lone tear crawling down her cheek. "I love our birthdays together, Mel. But yeah. This is special." She turns to her guy and the look that they share melts me on the spot. "Thank you, Jason."

Just then, Penelope walks in and sits at the end of the table, "Don't thank him until you've tasted the cake. It's Mary's specialty."

And right on cue Matthew's stomach growls, a sheepish look taking over his face as Jason chuckles. "Ladies, this is Matthew Crown. I believe he's the only one you haven't met yet."

I'm not sure who he's talking to, but his eyes haven't left my best friend and I couldn't be happier for the pair.

And because life is a bitch, Catherine's snark breaks into their moment. "So how do you all know each other?"

Before I can say anything, Maverick answers first, "Melissa is my best friend's little sister."

"You mean Erickson?" Jack, the eldest of the brothers, asks.

Maverick nods. "That'd be the one."

Right then, Catherine's eyes bore into Mila, wanting

more info. "Okay, but how did you not know of the Crown brothers? If you two knew Hunter, then clearly, you'd know about his family."

Who the fuck is Hunter?

I'm looking around the table, wondering if I've missed a brother, but all eyes are on Maverick. *Maverick,* who's looking guiltier than a dog covered in cat shit.

Oh, fuck no. I can't bite back my response. "She didn't know he was Hunter, let alone a Crown. My brother introduced him as Maverick, so that's what he's gone by. And whenever I would ask him for his real name, he'd either say it didn't matter or quote the dictionary for me, giving me some bullshit definition about how he's independent and doesn't go along with the crowd."

Catherine rolls her eyes. "I could see why he'd do that. They *are* Crown men, after all."

This just serves to piss me off even further. I don't give a shit if he were the Queen of Sheba. After all that we've been through, I'd think that I should at least know his real name.

But apparently, I'm not worthy of even that.

And if Catherine's words weren't, enough salt on the wound, Penelope's drive in the dagger. "Yes. They've had thirsty women after their deep pockets for as long as I can remember."

Oh, this is some shit. I've heard enough.

"Is that it? Is that why you refused to give me your name? Even after the cabin, you *still* didn't give it to me.*"* I push my chair back from the table, the loud scraping against the floor preceding the continuation of my verbal assault. "I can't believe that's what you think of me. That all I'd care about was your money instead of who you really are. What you were... *my hero*."

Those last two words get stuck in my throat, my chest getting impossibly tight as my eyes burn with impending tears. I need to get the hell out of here. Right the fuck now.

Without looking back, I hightail it out, not caring that I'm making a scene. Mila knows I'd make an even bigger one if I remained in the same room as that coward.

I can't help it—tears drip down my face as my heart implodes. *All this time.* All this fucking time. I loved him with everything I had, and he couldn't even give me his name.

No, there's no excuse. He doesn't want me, and it's never been clearer than it is right now. As I blindly open a door, quickly crumpling behind it, I know there's no other way. I have to leave. Leave this godforsaken town and get as far away from *Hunter* Crown.

Hunter

I've fucked up. Fucked up bad.

This is so much worse than my pushing her away at the cabin or the truck. And as I storm through the house, ripping every door open in search of my girl, I fear I've gone too far.

Damn it. Where is she?

I'm about to tear this house down when I hear the cadence of Mel's voice, but the pain in it slays me where I stand. I did that. *Me.*

A mixture of guilt and resolve comes over me as I approach the last door in the hallway, and that's when I hear it, the words that have my knees threatening to give out.

"Because I'm leaving this hell forsaken state and never coming back." Mel's voice cracks on that last word and my heart goes right along with it.

"Like fuck you are." A growl rips from me as I storm into the room.

"*Excuse me?*" Mel's eyes widen, her perfect pout parting in surprise, and if looks could kill, I'd be six feet under.

At least she's stopped crying as she gets up from the bed, charging toward me like a woman on a mission. Unfortunately for her, I'm about to show her who's in charge.

"You heard me, *baby doll.*" I step forward, closing the small gap between us, letting our bodies brush against one another as I stare my little girl down. "You aren't going anywhere."

Mel's breath hitches, her nipples hardening into points

against the thin shirt on my abdomen. "I don't have any reason to stay. Not when my best friend is leaving for college and my brother is always working. So, tell me, why should I stay?"

Placing both hands around her tiny waist, I dig my fingers in deep. "Because I said so."

Despite the shiver that dances across her perfect skin, Mel throws her head back and cackles. "Oh please. Says the man who wouldn't even trust me with his name. That's hilarious."

Her body is shaking in my hold, but I'm not deterred. Yes, I fucked up. But I'll be damned if I let that mistake keep us apart.

"I'm not joking, Melissa."

Something flares behind her eyes just then, a fire I've only seen once before. "Neither am I, *Hunter*."

Fuuuuuck. My body hums with pleasure. Just the mere sound of my name coming off of those fuckable lips has me craving more.

I want her screaming it. Screaming my name before I shove myself down her pretty throat.

Out of my periphery I see my girl's roommate stand, prompting Mel's response. "No, Mila. Stay. It's Maverick who needs to leave."

And just like that, I crave to hear my real name. Need it. Nothing else will do. "You're out of your goddamn mind if you think I'm leaving you alone right now."

Without skipping a beat, Mel responds. "And why is that?"

I'm pulling her harder into me, her neck arching back in order to look me in the eyes with so much vehemence, I almost believe the venom behind her words. Almost. But I know her like I know the back of my hand and I can see her wheels turning with every passing second, the thoughts making me chuckle.

"Because you're hell bent on punishing me, and god knows what you'll do if I let you."

Mel's mouth hangs open, her eyes going wide. "Yeah? Well, you'd deserve it, too… whatever it is that I'd do."

No doubt I do, but I'm not agreeing with her on that. Doing so would be signing away any hope of keeping my fiery girl, and that's just not something I'm willing to do.

"I have a better idea." Lifting Mel off the ground, I throw her over my shoulder and walk us out of the room.

"Put me down, you fucking caveman!" Melissa's fingernails scrape against my back as she shouts, but it does nothing but make my cock hard. "Mila! Stop him!"

"Oh, no. I'm not getting involved." I hear her roommate laugh behind us. Good. She knows it'd be pointless if she did.

"Traitor!" Melissa yells as she lets her body go limp against mine, and if I'm not imagining it, she curls herself in, pushing herself closer against me.

That's right, baby. You know who this body belongs to. *It's mine.* All mine.

But the truth is, I belong to her too. Every bit of me has always been hers, and maybe it's about damn time I stopped denying it.

Chapter Nine
MELISSA

"Where are you taking me?!" I'm screeching as Hunter carries me through the woods. A norm for us, it seems.

"My cabin on the property."

"You can't just keep taking me like this, Hunter. I'm not a possession. I'm a human being." He grunts at this but says nothing more. "I'm serious!"

"So am I." He takes a few more steps before he's lowering me onto the ground. "Look, I fucked up. I admit it. I should've told you my real name a long time ago."

I'm so taken aback by his admission that I'm momentarily stunned into silence. Thankfully, Hunter keeps talking and what he says next has my knees threatening to give out.

"I know what you are. Who you are. Rare. Special. Everything a man could ever hope to want." He squeezes his eyes shut as he throws his head back, a meaty hand running through his hair. "Unfortunately for me, I had no business claiming you. I still don't. But that doesn't change the fact that you deserved nothing but the truth from me and for that, I am sorry."

I mean, *what do you say to that?* I have no fucking clue. All I know is that my legs are jelly, and my heart is about to beat out of my chest.

"Okay, then." Hunter nods as if I'd responded, his towering frame crouching down once more before he's carrying me over his shoulder. "The cabin is only a few feet away. As soon as we get there, I'm drawing you a bath and making you dinner. We didn't eat at the house and you're going to need the energy for what I have in mind."

I swallow thickly, the images his words conjure instantly giving me the taco tingles. *Holy-fucking-shit.* It doesn't matter. I *will not* give in to him. He's hurt me more than once and being intimate like that with him again will only serve to wreck me. *I just know it.*

I'm about to tell him as much when we're stepping into a small clearing, and from my vantage point I see it—the gorgeous A-Frame cabin. But instead of going inside, we go around to the back and I'm stunned speechless once more.

There's a beautiful outdoor shower area, complete with a soaking tub looking out into the setting sun, lighting the entire area in this ethereal pink glow. I haven't even fully soaked in the scenery when Hunter issues his first command.

"Get naked," A thundering voice booms, the two words alone making my entire body shiver.

Oh, boy. He can order me all he wants, but it doesn't mean I'm giving in.

Bracing myself before I turn, I see that Hunter is running the bath, the sight alone threatening to make me cave. *Be strong, girl. He hurt you.*

Okay, if he's going to tease me with what I can't have, then I'll just have to do the same. Deliberately slow, I unbutton the front of my cotton dress, all while keeping my eyes trained on his. "Yes, Sir."

My words have their desired effect, making this beast of a man shudder in response. "Fuck, baby. Talk to me like that and we won't get to dinner."

"Hate to break it to you, my feral Buddha, but I haven't agreed to anything. Especially any pre or post dinner activities." I raise a brow as I let the cotton dress drop to the ground, watching as the inky black dots in Hunter's eyes swallow the flecks of gold and green. "What? Does daddy like what he sees?"

Hunter's jaw clenches, his chest visibly rising and falling as one of my hands goes to the clasp on my bra. "Oh, Daddy likes."

In one swift move, he's up, ripping the material from my body before turning me around and giving me a swat to the ass. "But first, a bath. Then dinner…and maybe if I'm lucky, something else."

I'm still shaking my head no when he's lifting me off the ground and walking me over to the large tub. *Heaven.* That's what it feels like as he lowers me into the warm bath water, the soft waves it's making lapping at my breasts as I look over the setting sun. I might still be pissed as hell, but damn, what a view.

And just when I think this couldn't get any more perfect, Hunter places a lingering kiss on my forehead. "Get yourself nice and clean for me, baby. Daddy's gonna have so much fun getting you dirty."

And without another word, the man of my dreams turns, leaving me a confused pile of mush in the most beautiful setting of my life.

But hey, if I'm going to stew in my anger, this is definitely the place to do it in.

Hunter

The entire time I've been watching her eat has been torture. From the way she sucks off her spoon to the way she licks her lips—every damn thing has my dick throbbing in need.

"You know if you keep staring at me your face is going to freeze like that." Mel is glaring, thinking she's still mad at me.

I can't help but chuckle, but this only earns me a death glare from the wannabe ice queen. "What's so funny?!"

"Nothing, baby. You ready for dessert?"

Her eyes go wide before she schools her features. Yeah, I know what my baby likes. I've got a massive hole to dig myself out of, and chocolate should be a good start.

"Dessert?" She's giving me side eye, but her pink tongue pokes out as she licks her juicy bottom lip.

I nod, extending a hand and helping her stand. "It's outside. Thought I'd make my girl some s'mores on the fire pit."

We haven't made it two feet out the door when I hear it, her gasp.

While she was out back soaking, I laid out blankets and pillows, making sure the 'fairy lights,' as Penelope calls them, were on.

"You know..." The little brat places a hand on her hip before she cocks it to the side. "Just because you set this all up, making it look like something straight out of a Nicholas Sparks movie, it doesn't mean I'm forgiving you."

"I know, baby." I take a step closer to her, dropping my hands to either side of her hips before bringing her into me.

"I just thought my girl would enjoy a little sugar for the bitter conversation we're about to have."

This makes her head rear back, her crystal blue eyes searching mine. "Bitter? I'm not bitter. I'm mad. I'm sad. I'm just so disappointed."

It's the last two that dig a ridge the size of the Grand Canyon straight into my heart. *Fuck.* I really hurt her bad.

Clearing my throat, I take her hand and walk her toward the fire pit. "Okay… how about we start with the disappointed."

It's the worst of the bunch, so we might as well rip the Band-Aid off.

With visible hesitation, Mel nibbles on her bottom lip before settling between two large pillows. "I guess, I've just always seen you as this larger-than-life person. *Unshakeable. Unwavering.* And when you abandoned me for the second time, after we did what we did in the cabin… It just felt like, you knew what you wanted while we were doing it, but then completely flipped and flaked as soon as the light of dawn hit."

A lump forms in my throat. I can't believe she thinks my feelings for her are so flippant. "Mel, baby—"

"No. I'm not done," *Oh god.* I brace for impact as a lone tear rolls down her beautiful cheek. "And then, if that weren't enough, I find out that you've been keeping your real name from me because you thought I was some gold-digging ho. It's bullshit. All I ever wanted was your time and attention, and you couldn't even give me your name!"

She's fuming now, her body vibrating in place as her face flushes pink under the moonlight.

"Stop right there." I take hold of her waist, lifting her up and settling her on top of me. Thankfully, she doesn't fight me... although if looks could kill, I'd probably be laid out. "I, under no circumstances, have *ever*, and I mean *ever*, thought you were some gold-digging ho."

Her eyes narrow as she full-on pouts. "Explain."

I can't help but bite back a smile, my hand reaching for the bag of candy I'd stashed nearby. "Okay. But first, try some of this."

Mel's eyes go wide. "Oh my god, this fudge, it's from Casey's on Main Street."

I nod, my focus trained on her luscious lips as she licks them in preparation of the chunk I've just broken off. "Sure is, baby doll."

"But, how'd you know?" Her brows are furrowed as she searches my face.

"That it's your favorite? Because, like I said, I've never thought of you as something other than goddamn perfect. My perfect baby doll with a penchant for candy." Taking the piece I'd broken off, I slowly bring it to her mouth—my cock instantly rising to its full length as soon as her lips wrap around my fingers.

Yup, I'm a goner as soon as her soft-wet tongue swirls around them, sucking off every morsel as visions of exactly what that mouth could do flood my brain.

"Mmmm." Mel licks her lips in appreciation. "Perfect, every single time."

"Just like you, baby. Just like you." I swipe across her fat bottom lip, my eyes trained on how the supple flesh gives under my touch. And I can't help it, I give it a slow shove inside, watching as the meaty digit disappears into her wetness.

Damn, that's hot. Adding fuel to the fire, Mel swirls her tongue around me, making my cock lurch in my pants, the fucker wishing it were him getting this attention.

I'm about to shove my girl down when she raises a brow, a devious smirk playing on her lips as she pulls me out of her mouth. "Oh, no. Don't think you get to feed me a little chocolate and you're off the hook. You still haven't explained." She squirms a little and I know the moment she feels it, the bulge in my pants. Her face transforms from furious to shy then back to furious, all in a span of two seconds. But after regaining her composure, she issues her demand once more. "Go on. Explain."

Chuckling, I comply. "Honestly, at first it was just out of habit. But as you got older and started blossoming into a woman I could no longer ignore, it sort of became a sense of self-preservation." Mel's eyes are intent on me, and I know she still doesn't get it. "Look, I was already following you around all the time. You consumed every thought, from the moment I woke up to the moment I went to bed. *'Was Mel okay?' 'Did she eat enough?' 'Did any customers give her shit?'* Non-stop thoughts of how your day-to-day had gone and whether or not I needed to kick anyone's ass."

Melissa's jaw drops, her mouth opening and closing a couple of times before she's able to form words again. "But... you didn't have to do any of that. Not even my own brother goes through such trouble."

I scoff. "And that's exactly why. Your father is a piece of shit—*no offense*—and Eric? Well, he's always been lost in his own world. You needed someone looking out for you, and fuck if I'd let it be anyone other than me."

Tears are welling up in my girl's eyes and I don't know if they're good or bad. "You really are my Daddy, aren't you?" She's sniffling now, her bottom lip trembling.

"You have no idea, baby. No fucking clue." I swipe at her tears with both thumbs, cradling her face with my hands. "All that worrying turned into a sick and twisted obsession. In my head, you were mine. My baby doll." I throw my head back as a sardonic laugh rumbles from my chest. "Unfortunately for you, I'm one fucked up Daddy. The things I thought of doing to you... the things I want to do to you. I couldn't taint you like that. Muck you up with all of my filth."

Melissa shoves at my chest. "That isn't your choice to make! It's mine!"

I'm taken aback by her words, because they're true.

"You're right." I close my eyes and breathe in the air

around us, a mixture of Mel's peaches and cream scent and summer nights—an intoxicating combination.

Before I let it take me under, I lift Mel off my lap, much to her confusion, and start on the fire.

"Wait... so that's it? You're just going to agree with me?" She's standing up, her arms folding in front of her as the fire roars to life.

"Yes." I turn to look at her face in the amber glow and my breath is stolen right from its lungs. *Fuck, she's beautiful.* "You're right. But so am I. We both have a choice, and my choice has been to protect you. Unfortunately, I failed you once, keeping you safe from everything but myself. And I'm telling you now, that will always be the case. Even if it means having to bend the truth just to keep you from harm."

Her mouth drops open as her big eyes blink up at me, but no words escape. Unable to help it, I bring my lips down to hers and slowly drink her in. She tastes of chocolate and sin, my new favorite flavors.

Taking a step closer into her space, I press our bodies together, needing the contact now more than ever.

"Wait..." She pushes me back. "So, you're saying that you're going to keep lying to me, and I could either take it or leave it?"

"Only when it's a matter of keeping you safe." Her brows drop and eyes narrow, and I know she doesn't understand. "Mel, as badly as I want between these legs," I drop a hand, trailing it up her exposed thigh before hovering it right over her heat. "It will always be your choice."

"My choice…" Mel's eyes gloss over as a whimper falls from her lips.

"Yes. Your choice." And I'm not making it an easy one as I let my thumb slowly stroke between her slit, teasing her with what she could have. "So, what's it gonna be, baby doll? Does my girl want to stop, or does she want to play?"

Chapter Ten
MELISSA

I'm standing. Right? I think I'm still standing.

A shudder wracks my body as Hunter's calloused hand trails up my thigh, his fingers softly tracing my damp slit. "So, what's it gonna be, baby doll? Does my girl want to stop, or does she want to play?"

I'm a confused pile of mush as his words ring in my head. Part of me wants to forgive him already, but another part of me is scared to. Scared to open up to him once more just so he could let me down whenever he decides he knows what's best.

Fuck that. If that's how he wants to playthings, then I plan on making it as difficult as possible for him.

"Oh, we can play. But since you just want what's best for me, then you have to prove it... only I get my release."

Hunter's chuckle is dark as I wonder just what I've gotten myself into. "Oh, baby doll. Giving you pleasure is a gift in and of itself." He prowls closer, his eyes soaking me in before his strong hands go to the cleavage of my dress. "If that's your only condition, then I agree."

"Yes, that's my only condition." I swallow thickly, but the lump in my throat goes nowhere.

And Hunter doesn't hesitate, he's ripping my dress in two, the white cotton fabric falling to either side of my body as he stares at what he's just uncovered.

Holy shit.

"Perfection, baby. That's what you are." His hands go to my breasts before his thumbs slowly flick my pert nipples, each pass sending a jolt of lightning straight between my thighs. "These tits, the most beautiful thing I've ever seen."

I have no words. I can't respond. His hands on my body are like a drug, one that's taken me over and left me hungry for more.

"Goddammit, baby. I can see those hard little nipples right through the lace." He slaps at the side of my breast and it jiggles before him. "Such a bad girl, teasing Daddy with these perky little tits. They're just begging for attention, aren't they?"

Needing no prompting, Hunter lowers his mouth to one of the fleshy mounds, wrapping his lips around one of the stiff peaks and soaking the fabric straight through as he suckles. *God, that feels so good.*

"Yes, Daddy. I'm so bad." I moan, thrusting my chest higher. "Looks like you'll just have to teach me a lesson."

Hunter raises a brow before a wicked smirk touches his full lips. "Okay, baby. But remember, you asked for it."

Before I'm able to ask what he means, he's ripping the lace from my body, my breasts now exposed under the light of the moon.

"*Jesus*, I'm going to have so much fun with you." Hunter bites his fat bottom lip before he's whirling me around and placing me on all fours, a swat to the ass the last thing I feel before I hear him by the fire. "Keep your eyes on the ground, baby. Daddy's orders."

There's the rustling of a wrapper and the clanking of a metal poker, and I just have to ask, "Are you making dessert?"

"No, sweetheart." I feel him kneel down behind me, one of his calloused palms running over the globes of my ass. "You're the only thing I'm eating up tonight."

Oh god. My body comes to life as Hunter rubs something hot and sticky from the base of my neck down to my puckered hole.

"Wha—What is that?"

My man chuckles as he positions his body behind mine,

his hand going to the nape of my neck before it's wrapping around my hair and yanking—*hard*.

"Marshmallow. Almost as sweet as your cunt. Almost."

I don't get a chance to respond because Hunter's mouth descends on my heated flesh, his mouth licking a path down my body until one of his hands is squeezing the cheek he'd just smarted moments ago.

"Fuck, baby. Even your tight little ass is perfect." He's releasing his grip on my hair, only to bring both hands to either cheek, his fingers digging in before he's pulling them apart. "And that little pink rose, it's teasing me, begging to be filled."

I whimper, remembering the last time we were together. He played with me then, and I'd be lying if I said it didn't feel good.

"That's right, doll. I know what you like."

Just then I shudder, feeling his warm wet tongue circle the object of his rapt attention. God, why does that feel so good, and why do I want more?

As if reading my mind, Hunter pushes inside, his tongue spearing through me and making me moan. "Oh, Daddy. So good."

But just as quickly as he started, he stops, leaving me bereft and clenching for more. "Wha—Why did you stop?"

Hunter smacks my ass, the force of it making the flesh sting. "My greedy little girl. So hungry for Daddy."

"Yes!" I wiggle my ass in the air, hoping to bring him back to me. "Now give me more."

"No. Only good girls get to cum. Bad girls get tortured and teased—tantalized until they're nothing but a squirming, writhing mess—just begging for release. And then, only then, do they get their reward." He lifts his hands to my breasts, his thick fingers tweaking the already sensitive nubs and making me cry out in pleasure.

Mid scream, Hunter flips my body over like a rag doll, throwing me down on the pillows beneath.

Shit, I'm already a squirming, writhing mess, but I'm not about to admit it. Especially not with the tortured look on Hunter's face. *Good*. At least I'm not the only one left wanting more.

Hunter bends over me and that's when I see it, the sticky marshmallow he's bringing down on my breasts. With slow methodical movements, this beast of a man spreads the white sweetness over both peaks, making sure to flick each nipple twice, the act making me arch from pleasure with every pass.

I can't help it, my chest heaves as I close my eyes from the overwhelming sensations, but it's nothing compared to the feeling of his soft tongue rubbing against my hard nipples, his entire mouth sucking as I curse his name.

"More, Daddy. Please." I'm whining, not giving a shit that I'm breaking beneath him. I need more, and I need it now.

"Does my baby need to be filled? Is her pretty little pussy crying for attention?"

I'm nodding as Hunter drops his mouth over my mound, my lips clinging to the fabric as the evidence of my desire soaks through.

"Too bad. I'd love nothing more than to shove my cock deep inside that wetness, but my little girl said I couldn't get off."

My mouth drops open in disbelief that he's actually going to deny me.

"*But I need it.*" I'm pouting and I don't give a shit. "I need Daddy's cock."

Hunter *tsks* as he leans back on his legs. "Rules are rules, and I'm not going to break them."

I'm about to start protesting again when out of a bag he's pulling out a long twisting lollipop, the kind that look like a unicorn's horn, and instantly my heart starts racing. "What's that?"

"You can't have Daddy's cock, but you can have the next best thing." My jaw drops for what feels like the millionth time as Hunter pushes my thighs open, his body settling between. "I need you to play with those gorgeous tits, baby. Can you do that for me?"

I nod but lose the ability to speak as soon as Hunter waves the long piece of candy in front of my slit, using the tip to nudge the elastic of my panties to the side.

"Don't stop, baby. Tug on those hard little nipples for me."

My eyes roll back as I do what he says, the sensation of

my hands and the blunt tip of the candy on my bare flesh sending me over the edge as I moan out in pleasure.

Increasing his torture, Hunter presses the hard tip against my clit, slowly swirling it around and making my hips pivot right along with it. *Holy fuck.* It's so much, yet not enough.

"More," I beg, my voice coming out hoarse and unrecognizable. "Please. I need you inside."

Hunter chuckles as he slowly glides the candy up and down, up and down, all in a torturously slow movement. "You're such a good girl, getting nice and wet for Daddy."

"Yes, so wet. So ready." I'm delirious, shaking my head from left to right, needing to feel something, anything inside of me. "Please."

"God, I love it when you beg. It makes me want to give you the world." His words shock me into submission, and I have no snarky response. This seems to please him because he *finally* gives me what I want.

With one swift thrust, Hunter shoves the lollipop inside, my body instantly jolting from the intrusion. I should object, I should push him away—it's a fucking candy he's just shoved inside my pussy—but I don't.

Like a wanton whore, I writhe against it, needing even more still. *I'm literally riding a damn lollipop, chasing my release.* And fuck if the thought of that doesn't help me get off.

"Such a horny little thing." Hunter slowly thrusts in and

out, tilting the long swirl just right so it's pressing against a spot that has me seeing stars.

"What—what are you doing to me?" The slow and steady pressure against my inner wall has my body shaking, my legs losing all strength as they flail to either side.

Hunter's dark chuckle makes a return, but I can't even muster the strength to look at his face. I'm lost in this sensation, the entire world burning up around me as this fire consumes me whole.

"That's your g-spot, baby." He applies more pressure then, and the fire grows dark. Everything around me fades and the only thing I see is nothing but black. "That's it, baby. Let it take you over."

My walls are clenching around the stick, spasming and milking it as if it were my Daddy's big cock.

God, how I want that.

"Damn, baby. Such a greedy pussy, getting this candy nice and juicy for me." Right then Hunter brings his mouth down onto my heated flesh, his tongue lathing at the sensitive bundle of nerves and I shatter.

His mouth paired with the mental image of Hunter sucking on the lollipop I'd sullied has me crashing hard into my release. It's unlike anything I've ever felt as wave after wave of pleasure washes over me, I'm not sure it will ever stop.

As if reading my mind, Hunter shows no sign of stopping, his tongue swirling around my engorged clit and showing it no mercy.

With one final shudder, my hands finally fall from my breasts and go to Hunter's hair, feebly attempting to push him away. This man has wrecked me. Here I thought I was teaching him a lesson when the only thing that's happened is that I now know I'd never want to live without him or the pleasure he's able to give.

Well played, Hunter Crown. Well played.

Chapter Eleven
MELISSA

I'm still drunk off my orgasm when something vibrates, the sound pulling me out of my bliss-induced stupor.

My eyes are barely open, but out of my periphery I see Hunter pull a small glowing phone out of his pocket.

"Hello?" There's a pause but his body says it all. It's gone ramrod straight and his moonlit face speaks of violence. "Yes. Have you called the men of WRATH?" More silence as Hunter puts out the fire we'd just been enjoying. "Right. We're on our way."

Before I've even had a chance to ask what's going on,

Hunter is at my side wrapping me up in a blanket like a burrito. "We're going to the main house."

"And? You can't just whisk me away after an ominous phone call like that. I need details." I'm shoving at his chest but he's already carrying me through the woods.

"You're not going to like it."

"Hunter…" I admonish. "You can't make these types of decisions on your own. Not when they might involve me. Yes, you might've rescued me as a clueless teenager, but I'm no longer her."

"Oh, trust me." His eyes briefly meet mine before they're back on the trail. "I've noticed."

This makes me smile as I remember our tryst under the stars, but it's quickly quashed by Hunter picking up speed. "What is it? What's going on."

"We can't linger on the path."

Oh god. That doesn't sound good.

"Is something out there? Someone?"

"Don't worry, baby doll. Nothing will touch you. I'd tear them limb from limb before they'd hurt a hair on that pretty head."

A lump forms in my throat, my swallowing now becoming difficult. I don't doubt Hunter's words for a second. This man is fiercely protective, but that doesn't mean I'm not scared for his sake.

"Please, don't say that. I can't stand the thought of something happening to you. Especially not because of me."

Hunter scoffs. "Don't you get it, baby doll? I'd slay a million men if it meant you'd be safe. And do you know why?"

"No." I shake my head.

"Because my world would cease to spin without you in it. You're the reason my sun rises and moon sets. You're the best part of this wretched life, and making sure you remain here, with me, is worth each and every sacrifice."

Speechless. I'm once again left without words.

Who'd have thought that this stoic man would have the power to render me silent? *Not me.*

"We're about to hit the clearing and being out in the open isn't any better." He adjusts my position on his body, throwing me over his shoulder in a maneuver so smooth I wonder how many times he's done this before. "On the count of three, we're sprinting. Hang on, baby doll. It's going to get bumpy."

Much like the state of my heart. Just when I'd thought there was no hope for us, this man goes and says things that make me think of forever.

And as we rush toward the main house, I can't help but send up a silent prayer, wishing with all that I have for this to be it—*our very own happily ever after.*

"WHAT DO YOU MEAN THEY SHOT MILA?!" I'M

screeching, barely able to contain myself from running out the door and in search of my best friend.

"You aren't going anywhere, baby." Hunter's strong hands press down on my shoulders, effectively keeping me on the family room's couch.

I'd been with Penelope, changing into some borrowed clothing, so this is the first I've heard of what's going on.

"No, you can't just tell me my best friend has been hurt, or worse, and then tell me I can't go see her." I go to get up once more, but Hunter keeps me down, his words only soothing me the slightest bit.

"She's safe, Melissa. We've called the doc and he'll be running some labs, but there's no visible point of entry which makes us think it was a dart of some kind."

"*A dart*? Where the fuck are we, the Amazon?"

Hunter releases a hand, bringing his fingers to the bridge of his nose and squeezing. "We're trying to figure out who's behind it, but I suspect we already know."

That last part is said under his breath, making me think it wasn't for me. "Okay... That's all good and gravy, but I want to see my friend."

"I know, baby." Hunter's eyes land back on me, and I can't quite place the look on his face. "I promise you, she's in good hands. Jace is with her, and as soon as the men of WRATH have finished securing the area, I'll take you for a visit."

Just then, Mary hands me a hot cup of tea. "Here you

go, darlin'. I know coffee is more our speed, but I thought you could use something a little more calming right now."

"*Mmm.*" I hum as notes of chamomile and honey dance on my tongue. "Thank you, Mary. This means so much."

The corner of her eyes crinkle as she smiles down at me. "Of course, sweetheart."

And if this moment couldn't be any more overwhelming, Penelope and Anaya arrive with bags in tow, the pregnant brunette being the first to speak up.

"We've been down this rodeo before. Thought we'd get you set up for a week at the very least."

I'm blinking up at them as a mixture of gratitude and fear floods through me. *Wait, what did she just say?*

"A week?" My head flings back to Hunter who's on the phone, but nods at the girl's assessment.

"At the very least." The blonde, Anaya, chimes in. "God, didn't you go missing for a whole month before they were able to track you down in Mexico?" She's looking over at Penelope like she'd just asked when her last hair appointment was, not a damn kidnapping.

My heart is racing as insane thoughts flood me. "Hold on, is someone trying to take out Mila?!"

"Breathe, baby. Everything is going to be okay." Right then, Hunter comes and sits by me, his open palm rubbing slow circles on my back. "We'll be going on lockdown. Just ironing out the logistics."

"Lockdown?" My eyes go wide and the cup in my hand

shakes, spilling some of the liquid on my lap and burning the inside of my thigh. "*Shit!* I'm so sorry."

Hunter swipes at it, his touch soothing me more than he knows. "Shhh. It's just a little spill."

"But the couch, it's dirty now."

Hunter raises a brow. "Give us enough time and I promise you, one way or another this couch would be filthy."

The hidden meaning isn't lost on our company and while the girls giggle, our new visitor doesn't.

"Get your fucking hands off my sister." Eric enters the room with a growl, his eyes laser focused on where Hunter's hand still lays.

Beside me, Hunter's chest vibrates, a grunting sound his only response, his hand unmoving.

Choosing to ignore this exchange, I ask the obvious. "Eric? What are you doing here?"

Thankfully, my brother takes the diversion. "I got a call that it was all hands on deck. Besides, I have news…"

At this, Hunter's body tenses. "Did you get eyes on the perp?"

"No, but we did find tracks. It seems—"

"Oh, God! Here you all are! Where's my Mila? I can't find her anywhere, and I was just told we're in lockdown!" The Wicked Witch is here to steal the show with her dramatics. *Typical.* "She was so upset at the dinner, I just wanted to check in on her. Make sure she's okay."

Hunter's eyes narrow, his eyes assessing. "She's with my brothers now. There's been an incident."

"An incident?!" Catherine's hands fling to her chest, her feet stumbling back and making her land against my brother. "What sort of incident?"

"She passed out in the woods earlier," Eric answers behind her, his words making her features soften a little.

"Oh, heavens. I thought you were going to tell me something worse." She rights herself, her hands smoothing down her dress. "That girl never eats enough. Always starving herself for men and attention."

"That's a fucking lie and you know it!" I'm shouting, the damn teacup spilling over once more in my agitation.

"Here, darlin.' Let me take that from you." Mary reaches to take the cup from my hand, but Hunter stops her, his head shaking and eyes knowing. *How? How does he know what sets me off?* It's like he's in tune with what makes my demons come to life, the fuckers dragging me under and taking me into their dark abyss.

"Potato, tomato. That's neither here nor there, Melissa." The witch spits out, downplaying her blatant lie. "If that's all it is, why is there a lockdown?"

"First of all, that's not how the saying goes," Eric sneers. "Second of all, there's more to it but the information is on a need-to-know basis."

This makes Catherine's face blanch.

"He's right," Hunter agrees beside me. "First thing's first. We need to figure out the housing situation."

"But not after I marry the woman of my dreams," Austin announces as he enters the room, his piercing green eyes landing on his bride-to-be, Anaya.

Turns out there's going to be a wedding on the family ranch, although I'm not sure if that's still going forward.

As if in answer to my question, Anaya chimes in. "Please, if it isn't safe then we can just wait."

Her fiancé chuckles behind her, his arms wrapping around the blonde's waist. "Honey, if we waited on the dust to settle, we'd be waiting forever—and that's not something I'm willing to do. I need to make you mine. *Now.*"

"Okay, you two. Keep it PG." Pen snickers, but this only earns her a swat to the ass from the other Crown brother who's just entered the room.

"You're one to talk, Princess." Jack purses his lips at her before he's turning to look at the engaged couple. "We can secure the property, but the location will need to change and the reception will have to be held elsewhere."

The couple nods in agreement, but it's Catherine who speaks up first. "And after that? Are we allowed to leave?"

Jack snorts. "You aren't a prisoner, lady. All I said was that you needed to wait until we got the all clear."

Catherine's face tinges pink. "I was just asking because Hunter had mentioned there being a 'housing situation.'"

"That only applies to the Crown women." The dig is obvious, and Catherine doesn't miss it. She isn't one of them, but then again, neither am I.

"So, then I can go too?" I turn to look at the man who's stolen my heart, unsure if I'm ready to leave his side.

Luckily, he answers without hesitation. "Over my dead-*fucking*-body."

"Happy to oblige, *brother*," Eric retorts without missing a beat, his words earning all eyes on him.

"Whoa. I don't know what's happened between you two, but fuck with our brother and you fuck with all of us, you hear?" Jack, the eldest of the Crown men takes a step toward Eric, making his intention crystal clear.

"It's all good, Jack," Hunter answers as he rises from the sectional we'd been sharing. "He's just got his panties in a wad because Mel and I are together."

My jaw drops as I go into shock. Hunter's just announced this to the room as if it's no big deal.

It is a big deal. A big fucking deal. And the stunned silence is a massive indicator that everyone else in the room thinks so too.

"This is news to me." I glare at Hunter who's just gone and made this decision for the both of us. Yes, I want him, but not if he's going to keep lying to me.

"Well, now you know." Hunter raises a brow before he's dropping a quick kiss to the top of my head.

"Oh, this conversation isn't over," I mutter under my breath just loud enough for him to hear.

And lucky for him, Jack claps his hands, breaking into the tense moment. "Alright then, now that we have that out in the open, let's talk rooming situations. We've got an all-hands meeting with the security team in ten."

"That's easy, my sister comes with me." Eric smirks, his feet taking him closer to Hunter, but stopping just shy of stepping on his shoes. "Your safe homes have both been compromised in the past. That's just not a risk I'm willing to take with Melissa."

"And *your* cabin is safer?" Hunter scoffs.

"Not the cabin you know of, but I've another location. A bunker." My brother raises a brow, his eyes on Hunter, completely missing the look of horror on my face.

"A bunker?! Oh, hell no. There's no way in hell you're dragging me down into a bunker." Just thinking of it now is giving me the creepy-crawlies.

"Stop being a baby, Mel. It's for your own good." My brother rolls his eyes but is quickly shut down by Hunter.

"Hey, don't talk to her like that." Hunter turns to look at me and I'm not sure I like the apologetic look on his face. "But if it clears inspection, then I think he's right Mel."

My jaw drops for what must be the millionth time today. "You have got to be kidding me."

Hunter turns to face me, his hands resting on either hip. "No, baby. I wish I were." He presses a kiss to my forehead, the sole act serving to soothe my tattered nerves. "But these men, the ones out there, they're merciless, and there's no way I'd risk you getting caught up in the mix."

I feel it—the sting behind my eyes and the burn in my chest. "You can't leave me now. I just got you."

"And you'll always have me, baby doll." I'm shaking when Hunter's arms wrap around me, his towering frame pulling me into a tight embrace. "But right now, we have some loose ends to tie up, and I just can't risk something happening to you."

"Listen to *your man*, sister," Eric spits from behind Hunter. "He's finally making some sense."

Not to me he isn't. But I have a feeling that no matter how much I fight it, this is one battle I'll never win. Hunter is a stubborn man, and once he's made up his mind, there's no moving that mountain.

Chapter Twelve
HUNTER

"Alright, so what are we dealing with here?" Austin's gaze lands on our eldest brother, Jack.

"So far, there's no trace of who did it, but based on the footprints left behind, we either have a small man or a woman." Jack's words have my hackles rising.

Security on the property is tight as it is. Something just doesn't smell right.

"The men of WRATH have been patrolling the area, and they haven't notified us of any breaches." Austin's eyes narrow as he brings a hand to his face, his fingers rubbing at the stubble on his jaw.

"So, what do you think?" I look toward our youngest brother, wondering if he has the same assessment I do? "There are only two new people on the property. Both of which are close to the target, and both of which would fit the print description."

Jace nods, knowing full well what I'm implying. There's a family secret we've been guarding, and he's the only one that holds the tangible proof.

What are the odds that it's his girl being targeted? The odds that the only ones who fit the print description are those closest to her as well?

"Jace, you'd be the best one to fill us in," Austin walks over to our youngest brother, clapping a hand on his shoulder. "Any clue why they'd want to hurt your girl?"

At this, Jace visibly bristles. "You mean just like they went after Blanca, your deceased wife? Or Anaya, your now fiancé?" Jace stands, heading straight for the bar. "Your guess is as good as mine, brother. What do these men want with the Crown women?"

"The common denominator? The Crown men." Matt rubs at his mouth, his eyes glossed over in thought. "But we still don't know what it is they've been after. Yes, we know our parents had dealings with *El Jefe*'s cartel. But they've all been taken out, haven't they?"

I step up, needing to keep Matt and the rest of my brothers away from the truth for as long as possible. "All but *El Jefe* and his brother. But we know where they are and there's no escaping their rival cartel's hold."

"Not unless it's through death," Jace adds, one of his brows arching as he smirks.

"Don't give Austin any ideas," Jack reprimands, making Matt laugh but his tone is dark.

"Ha! The one you have to worry about going all machete happy is Austin."

Oof. It wouldn't be our brother's first decapitation, and I doubt the memory is a pleasant one to conjure.

Unable to stay quiet, I speak up. "That was low, even for you, brother."

Austin shakes his head, raising both palms toward the room. "It's all good. I've got the love of a good woman and a shit ton of Matt's Tortured Crown Whiskey—the best healing agents in the world."

I raise a brow to this. He's full of shit. No woman—and certainly no booze—has the power to heal, but I leave it that, unwilling to stir the pot.

If he thinks he's, had it bad, I pray he never finds out what lurks deeper in the shadows.

"Alright, so what's the plan then? We can't keep the women on lockdown forever."

My brows go up at Jace's words, the thought of that sounding extremely tempting.

"Oh no, Hunter." Jack chuckles. "I see that look on your face. I highly doubt Ericson would be happy with you keeping his sister captive."

Matt snorts. "Yeah. Care to tell us what happened there? You two seemed so close. He was your best friend."

This makes Austin spit out some of the whiskey he'd been sipping. "Um, did you miss the part where he was banging Ericson's little sister? I know I wanted to murder Jack after I found out he'd been with Pen. Safe to assume that this new animosity has something to do with *that*."

I roll my eyes, not wanting to go down this road. "Let's just leave it at the Crown men having a penchant for the forbidden."

Smirking, I see all of my brothers nod except for Matt. "Speak for yourselves. I may have ninety-nine problems, but a taboo bitch isn't one."

"Watch it!" Jack roars, and I'm surprised Matt doesn't disintegrate on the spot from his stare alone. "Talk all the shit you want, but I will not have you disrespecting any of the Crown women. Lord knows they already get enough heat from the town gossip mill."

Raising a hand, Matt backs down. "My bad, brother. Didn't mean to offend."

I shake my head, needing to reign in this circus. "Enough of this. What's the plan."

"The men of WRATH are still trying to find out what the cartel wants with our family. Yes, we know our father had business dealings with them. But to our knowledge, they ended before they were run off the road."

Silence falls on the room, a darkness we've been carrying for the past five years resurfacing and taking over. Though we haven't been able to prove it, we know our parent's death is linked to *El Jefe's* cartel.

"Okay, but I vote that we also jump in on the search for truth." Austin takes a pull from his tumbler, letting the lip of the glass rest on his mouth a beat before he continues. "Cautiously, of course. I've learned my lesson."

"Have you?" Jack asks, brows raised.

"I second Austin's vote," Matt chimes in.

"Fuck it. What's life without a little adventure." Jace lifts his glass in cheers. "Count me in, too."

Jack and I exchange a knowing glance. These fools don't know the Pandora's box they're about to open, but I'm not sure there's any stopping it.

As if in agreement, Jack nods. "So be it then. We'll join in with the men of WRATH."

And with those fateful words, our future is sealed. I just pray history doesn't repeat itself and we don't end up in a ditch somewhere.

Three days later

"You can't be serious, Eric? How do you expect the two of us to share this space? I barely have enough room to breathe!" Mel is waving her hands inside the bunker, her arms practically touching either side of the narrow tunnel.

Wow, this really is a shit hole, but I don't dare say it out loud. I know that if I do, Mel will lose it and storm out of here, leaving her exposed to danger. *Not happening.*

Cutting into my thoughts, Eric's voice echoes through the tunnel. "Hey, this is just the entry point, the deeper we go, the bigger it gets."

"Why does that sound like a line you feed all the girls?" Mel snickers as we descend into the ground, the long pathway finally giving way to a living room of sorts.

"Keep that shit up, Mel and I'll make you sleep on the couch." Eric snaps back as he switches secondary lights on.

"Wait, there's only one room in this place?" Melissa spins in a circle before stopping with both hands on her hips. "Why can't I just room with Mila? She's down in Miami all by herself."

I step into her, placing both hands around her small waist. "Because she's the primary target, baby. There's no way in hell I'd risk you being close to her right now."

Mel's mouth is hanging wide open, the site making me want to take it, biting down on the juicy lips before soothing them with my tongue.

"So, I don't even get to talk to her?"

"You get one weekly call!" Ericson bellows from another room.

Taking advantage of the fact that it's just us, I bring my mouth down to hers, sucking in her bottom lip and lathing it with my tongue. *Fuck. She feels so good.* This one kiss alone has me hard as stone, my cock throbbing with the need to be inside her.

"Mmmph, does Daddy need his little girl?"

Fuck me. This woman has the power to bring me to my knees.

"You have no idea, baby doll. I need you bouncing on my cock, right the fuck now."

"Too bad I'm not your girl. Otherwise I'd let you." She bats her lashes at me, thinking she's being slick with her seduction.

"I don't know what delusion you're under, baby, but you're mine. Every bit of you." I cup her heat and give it a little squeeze. "And this pussy? Yeah, It's mine too."

Mel's eyes narrow but I don't miss the way her breathing kicks up and her pupils dilate. "The only way I'll ever be yours is if you promise to always tell the truth."

I take both hands and move them to her hips, squeezing the supple flesh before I'm giving her one hard thrust. "Agreed. I'll always tell you the truth…" I lift her up by her ass, wrapping both of her legs around my waist as I walk us to the rear wall. "As long as it doesn't jeopardize your safety."

My baby groans in frustration but it quickly turns into a moan as I grind against her slit, my cock already at full mast, begging for just a little taste of that sweet cunt.

"Hunter," Mel whines, her hips pivoting as she chases the high only our bodies can give. "Please, just agree already."

"Agree to protect you? Always." Lowering a hand, I rip her jean shorts open, the small metal button ricocheting against the buckle of my belt. "Agree to make you feel good? Always." I trace two fingers up her silky folds, loving the way she pushes herself against them. *My greedy girl.* "Agree to fill you up? Always." I thrust those fingers inside her heat, instantly feeling her squeeze around me.

"Oh, god." She arches her back, shoving her juicy tits in my face. Unable to help it, I lower my head and take one into my mouth, t-shirt be damned. "Fuck, Daddy. That feels so good"

Christ, how I love the sound of that.

Mel is writhing against me, my mouth latched on and working her tit right over the cotton fabric. It's fucking fantastic, but I need more. *I need her naked.*

"Tell me you want this, baby. Tell me now." I'm two seconds from ripping off her clothes, my dick is so painfully hard, it needs inside. "Your brother. He's in the other room, but I don't give a fuck. You tell me you want your Daddy, and I'll give you what you need—what we both need."

Mel's eyes lock on mine, a brow raising before her hands go to her full breasts, massaging and pushing the two mounds together—the sight alone making my mouth water.

And just when I thought this girl couldn't surprise me anymore, she goes and rips her shirt down, exposing the prettiest nipples I've ever seen.

"I need you, Daddy. I need your mouth right here." My angel takes a dusky pink nipple between her thumb and forefinger, rolling the distended tip back and forth, waving it like a damn red flag in front of a raging bull.

God, how I've missed these.

"Go on, baby. Feed me that gorgeous tit while I play with your pretty little cunt."

And without missing a beat, my girl cups one of her breasts before pushing it forward and bringing heaven right to my mouth. *Heaven.* That's exactly what this must be as my lips wrap around the dusky pink circle and my tongue lathes against the hard little nub.

"Yes, Daddy." Mel arches further into me, her hips pumping hard on my hand. "Suck. Just. Like. That."

Fuck. She's delicious.

Adding another finger to the mix, I pump faster and harder, getting her ready for my girth because there's no way in hell I'm not getting inside. I don't give a shit if her brother has to stand there and watch. I'm shoving myself inside that wet pussy if it's the last thing I do.

Squelching sounds mingle with our moans and I know my girl is more than ready. And needing to see just how messy I've made her, I finally release my hold on her breasts.

Perfection, that's what she is.

"Look at you, baby, taking my fingers so good. That greedy little pussy sucking them right up." I spread my fingers wide, making her moan at the fullness, but her thrusting never slows. "Yes, I think you're ready for Daddy's cock. What do you think?"

"Like fuck she is!" I turn to see Ericson standing at the

threshold, nothing but sheer horror painted across his face. "Put those things away, Mel!"

My old friend is covering his eyes, shielding his vision from Mel's beautiful breasts, and I can't help but scoff.

"Brother, you either get the fuck out of here or get a free show," I reach into my jeans and give myself a tug. "Because I'm not slowing down."

"Awe, fuck! Are you kidding me?!" His look of disgust is the last thing I see before Ericson retreats, slamming the bedroom door behind him.

I wasn't bluffing, I would've taken my girl, audience and all. I know it's wrong. *It's filthy.* But fuck if I care.

Looking into Mel's eyes, I see she wouldn't care either. We're lost in each other. Too far gone in this lust to turn back.

"Christ, you're beautiful." I soak in every inch of her—her swollen lips, glistening nipples and heaving chest. I want all of her all at once.

Mel smirks, her brow raising. "Are you just going to stand there or are you going to fuck me?"

I throw my head back and laugh, my girl knowing just what to say to get me going. "Oh, I'm fuckin' you alright."

Without hesitation, I grip fingers around my girth, guiding the swollen head to nirvana, only letting go once I'm safe and snug inside her wet hole.

"Shit, baby. *So. Damn. Tight.*" Just then, Mel squeezes around me, my vision blurring as she threatens to make me cum with just her words.

"So tight, and just for Daddy." She hits me with a one-two of emotion and sensation when her fingernails run down my back as she presses our bodies closer together, her small lithe one grinding and rolling against my much larger one.

"That's right, doll." I bite her neck as I pound into her, shoving her body up against the wall with each thrust. "These legs, they only open up for me."

"Yes, yes, yes!" She's shouting with every push of my hips, the prettiest of sounds coming out of her.

And as she clenches and shudders around me, I know my girl is close, and so am I. *I'm not sure how much more of this blinding pleasure I can take.*

Grabbing hold of her ass, I pull her tight little cheeks apart, a fat digit finding the puckered hole and teasing it open. As expected, my baby gasps and groans.

"*Gah!*" She shakes her head, eyes squeezed shut. "No, Daddy. You only get that if you give me what I want."

"Wrong, baby. I told you…" I gently press my way inside, Mel's eyes opening wide before they're rolling back in her head. "Every bit of you is mine. Mine to protect and mine to pleasure."

Our thrusting never stops, my digit now in sync with every push and pull as my girl's fingers dig into my shoulders. And like magic, my doll's mouth rounds into the prettiest 'O' her body bearing down on mine as her hips shake and shudder.

"There she is." I let her ride out her release for as long

as I can muster, but it doesn't take much more of her walls squeezing around me to have me spilling inside her, my chest vibrating as I roar out my release.

Together, we climax, reaching the pique of pleasure in each other's arms. And at this moment, I know, no other woman will do. She's my baby doll, my everything, and I'd rather die than have to live a day without her.

Chapter Thirteen
MELISSA

"I'm going to die in this hellhole, Mila! I won't survive it!" I fling myself back on the tiny bed, my arm swinging over my head as I press the SAT phone to my ear. I'm on my third week with Eric and these four walls that have me wanting to crawl out of my skin.

Thankfully, he leaves for eight hours a day, but that isn't cutting it anymore. "All I get is one walk every twenty-four hours, and even then, I'm being trailed, a slew of men covering my every move. I swear, I've got more security than the British Queen!"

Mila chuckles into the line. "I think that's a bit of an

exaggeration, but yes, I'm starting to feel that this is all a bit excessive. Between the Wicked Witch shacking up with the love of my life and knowing that they're having a baby together, I'm losing my mind. I mean do I really need to be here, in the same city as them?"

"So, you really decided to give up on the love of your life, giving him to Catherine on a silver platter?"

"He isn't an offering, Melissa. He's having a baby with her, the least I could do for the peanut's sake is respect that and let them be a family."

"But it didn't seem like he wanted to be a family with her at all. He wanted that with you."

"Well, we can't all have what we want, can we? Sometimes we need to make sacrifices and be the bigger person." My friend sounds like she's trying to convince herself more than she is me.

"Hey, if that's what makes you happy. But know that you're always free to change your mind. That man's heart belongs to you, and in my opinion, you two are just torturing each other."

Mila scoffs. "Torture? Torture is being followed twenty-four-seven with no sign of escape. This all seems pointless. After all, my labs all came back normal and they couldn't find any sign of what they thought might've been a dart…Hell, maybe I imagined the whole thing in the woods."

"Stop right there, girl. If this was all because of some

sex-induced hallucination, I'm going to strangle you—right along with Hunter for leaving me down here."

"Speaking of which, have you been able to talk to him?" My best friend asks, but there's something off with her tone.

"No…" Immediately, my heart works overtime. "Do you know something I don't? *Is he okay?*"

"I don't know. I heard some of the men in my detail saying that they hadn't been able to get a hold of him for an entire week."

"But that's normal for him, right? He always goes off-grid, doing his own thing." I'm biting on my thumbnail, now. Grateful for my friend's insight, but concerned nonetheless.

"Yeah, that's what some of them were saying." She pauses, a sigh ensuing the longest seconds of my life. "But the others, they think it might be something to do with a cartel. I haven't been able to get much info out of them, but I was able to snag a number for Hunter's SAT phone."

I sit upright on the bed, in disbelief that it's taken my friend this long to tell me this. "Mila! Why were you holding this back?!"

"I know you, Mel. You can become a little…*obsessive*. And seeing how you're locked up in the middle of nowhere, it might be a little more intense than usual."

I scoff, knowing she's one thousand percent right, but I'm not admitting to it. "That is *so* not true."

"Yeah. It is." She laughs. "And I'm not there to walk you down from hysteria hill, should you decide to climb it."

My eyes narrow, face scrunching in distaste. "Hey, I don't appreciate your lack of faith in me. What am I going to do with a little ol' number?"

Mila sighs into the phone. "For starters, if he doesn't answer, you'll start to run through all sorts of scenarios as to why he didn't pick up. *Is he in danger? Is he dead?*" There's a pause, and I feel it coming before she even says it. "Or, *Does he not want you anymore?*"

Like a tsunami, wave after wave of darkness takes me under, my mind swimming against the current as thoughts of the past fill my lungs.

'You worthless waste of space.'

'You just fuck everything up.'

'God, Mel. Can't you do anything right?'

My breathing kicks up and my chest tightens—It's imploding. Suffocating. Robbing me of my breath.

'No wonder your momma left. Least you could do is open up those legs and make us some money. Earn your keep or get the fuck out, little girl.'

"Mel!" My best friend sounds off in the distance, her voice like a lighthouse, calling in a ship to safe harbor. "Answer me or I'm calling your brother."

I choke on a sob, my hand flying to my heart in an effort to slow it down, but it's pointless. The feeling of despair is so great, the ache in my chest will never truly go away.

I thought I'd healed. That I'd made this part of me disappear, never to be felt again. Yet, here I am, on the precipice of falling once more.

"Melissa! Answer me!" My best friend is full-on screaming into the line, and it's enough to jolt me out of the trance I'd been under.

"Hey, I'm so sorry." My voice comes out hoarse, but at least I'm able to string a sentence together.

"You see!" Mila huffs into the phone, her breathing coming in labored. "That's why I didn't give you his number before."

"I know. I get it. But it's still my choice. Especially since this is the only hour I get to talk until next week."

I can practically see Mila gnawing on her lip as she decides whether or not to fork over Hunter's SAT phone info.

"I hate the very idea of this, Mel. I don't think this is good for you, and I don't want to see you get hurt."

Her words hit deep. I don't think I've ever had anyone care for me the way she does. It goes beyond whatever familial relationship I share with my brother.

We may've been birthed by different mothers, but that girl is as good as blood, if not better.

"Please, Mila?"

A second passes. And then another.

"Fine. But I don't give a shit about Eric's one hour rule. If you start to spiral, you give me a call. Promise me, Mel? It's the only way I'm giving you his number."

I take in a deep breath, knowing that I might just have to use that lifeline if it boils down to it.

"Okay. I promise. I will call you, regardless of my brother's bullshit rule."

"I mean it, Mel. Our time is almost up."

"So, stop wasting time and fork it over already."

"Fine. It's 546-978-5555." There's a pause before she continues. "God, I hope I didn't just make a mistake."

"Stop being so dramatic, Mila. It's going to be okay. I'm okay. Promise." Even as I spit the words out, I doubt them myself.

Truth is, these past three weeks have been horrible on my mental psyche. Being alone more often than not leaves you with a lot of time to think. A lot of time to self-reflect. And not everything that I've found has been pretty.

There's something to be said for burying your battle wounds so deep that it seems as if, just for a moment in time, they've disappeared—no longer a part of who you are. But the truth is, they're always there, lurking in the dark... waiting. Waiting for an opportunity to spring back to life and show you that they are in fact a part of you. That they've formed you, and as you arose from the ashes, they've molded your perception and trajectory in life.

The question is—when it's all said and done—do you like who and what you've become?

"Fine. But call me. I'm serious, Mel." My best friend's words bring me back down to earth, a centering force I'm forever grateful for.

"Thanks, babe. Love you."

"Love you, too. And call me. I mean it." She tacks on the last part for the millionth time, and I can't help but laugh.

"Okay, mom. Talk to you soon." I end the line before she adds any more demands.

Time is ticking on Eric's phone allotment, and I'd be lying if I said my fingers weren't itching to get a hold of Hunter. God, how I miss that man.

I'd gotten so used to his shadow trailing me that the stark contrast of its absence is jarring. And I don't like it. At all.

Needing to rip the Band-Aid of uncertainty off, I dial Hunter's number with shaky fingers, praying he isn't in some compromising location and that I've given him away. *He'd know to turn his phone off right?* Of course he would.

The line rings once, twice.

"This is Hunter—"

"Oh, thank God, you're okay!" I let out a massive sigh of relief, but it's short-lived.

"Of course I am. Why wouldn't I be?"

I haven't spoken to this man in three weeks, and *this* is how he responds? "Um, it's Melissa. I was just worr—"

"I know who this is. Why are you calling?" His question is so matter of fact; it makes me question my own sanity.

Did I imagine our night under the stars? Our quick romp in the room not ten feet away?

"Hunter?" My voice cracks and I feel my lip wobble. This doesn't feel right. It feels like my heart is being ripped right out of my chest.

"Melissa, I'm busy. If you have nothing to say, then I need to let you go." He sounds so unaffected, as if I weren't breaking on the other end of the line.

"Hunter, I—I—"

"You what, Melissa? Spit it out or get off the phone. Quit wasting my time."

That does it. My heart splinters into a million tiny pieces. The man I've loved for as long as I can remember is talking to me as if I don't matter. As if I'm nothing more than a nuisance to him. *Worthless. Worthless, Mel. Good for nothing, Mel.*

Fuck.

That.

Shit.

Fuck that shit right out the door.

"Motherfu—"

"Yeah, if that's all you have to say I'm letting you go. And Melissa? Don't call again." The line dies and I'm left wanting to die right along with it. *My heart?* It's nothing but a pile of dust—Hunter's words having charred whatever was left of it to begin with.

My body slides off the bed, the phone falling to the ground as I hit the wooden boards. *Why? What happened? What changed?*

My mind starts racing with thoughts I'd thought had

long been buried. *He saw you. The real you. Hated it. Just like your mom. Just like your dad.* Why? But why? *Because you're worthless. You're nothing but a waste of space.*

I can't breathe.

I can't.

Closing my eyes, I let it take over. The pain so deep, it's slicing me in two.

Giving into my feelings, I'm on the verge of decimation. But as I let myself fully feel every bit of it, something magical happens... *surrender*. Surrender to the knowledge that those are just feelings. They are not me, and I am not them.

Just then, flashes of memories flutter through my mind's eye. *Mila's laughter. The sun touching my skin. The leaves dancing before me—all in the prettiest shades of orange, yellow, and red.* My breathing stutters as more floods in. More of the light in this world. The light that, bit-by-bit, has the power to drive out all of the darkness threatening to take me under.

It's there, in the small moments like the taste of chocolate as it's hitting my tongue, or the pinks and purples of an amazing sunset, that life is made worth living for. Those moments are all mine. Given to me by mere virtue of being on earth.

I am here, those moments mine, and I'll be damned if I squander another second away. I am a warrior, and I am worthy. Fuck those who couldn't see my worth. Their perception has *nothing* to do with me.

With every bit of fire in my body, I fling the phone hard against the door, the hunk of plastic breaking just as my heart did minutes ago. Funny thing is, moving past the pain of shattering and onto complete surrender, *I'm now free.*

Wiping my tear-stained face, I rise. Rise from the ashes once more. Determined to live life to the fullest. For me—just for me—because I am enough.

Chapter Fourteen
MELISSA

It's been twenty-four hours since my second re-birth of sorts. I'm still walking on shaky legs, but the bite of Hunter's rejection isn't as sharp. *I can breathe now.*

Taking in my surroundings, I ground myself, focusing on every detail, making it high definition in my mind.

My daily walk is one I'm no longer taking for granted, using it to heal and mend my tattered heart. I take in a deep breath, letting the musty smell of damp leaves fill my lungs, the cracking of twigs a constant reminder that I'm being tailed, and I am not alone. *Never truly alone.* My new shadows are nothing like Hunter, but that's something I welcome right now.

They usually hide, keeping their distance, but because the past month has been anything but ordinary, one of them steps out from behind a massive tree.

"Ma'am. You have a visitor." The tall bodyguard is stoic, not a trace of emotion behind his features. "It's your father and someone Eric had cleared for visitation, but the choice is yours. Just give us the word, and we'll have him out of here in no time."

My father. A lump forms in my throat as my mouth fills with sawdust.

"Just one question. Is he sober?" I raise a brow, knowing that no matter how much healing I've done, I will not be facing that man if he's intoxicated.

"Yes, ma'am. He's sober." Again, no trace of emotion behind the bodyguard's face.

I suppose that's for the best. I've got enough for the both of us.

"Then it's fine. I'll see him." Knowing that this visit will probably devolve into an embarrassingly trashy one, I turn at the last minute. "But if you could give us some privacy, I'd really appreciate it."

The man's eyes narrow before they're flitting over my shoulder to something past me. He must see what he wants because he nods, his eyes landing back on mine. "Fine. But if you need us," He hands me a small cylinder that's attached to a lanyard. "Just press the button at the end."

The necklace of sorts is placed over my head, the plastic pendant hanging just between my breasts.

I feel it's unnecessary, knowing I've battled this man many times before, but I wear it anyway. He may be a dick, but he's never once overpowered me. I'm faster than he is.

"Fine." Turning back toward the tunnel, I descend into my hobbit hole, wondering what in the fuck old man Ericson wants this time.

But stepping into the main living space, my hand instantly swings to the pendant. *Something isn't right.* The entire space is trashed, it's been ransacked.

"*Dad?*" My voice shakes as I call out into the empty room, and it's a good two seconds before I get a response.

"There she is..." My father emerges from the sole bedroom, an evil grin plastered over his sweaty face. "The little whore."

"What's going on? Did you do this?" I'm cursing under my breath—I thought the monotone bodyguard said he wasn't inebriated.

"No, Casper the Friendly Ghost did it. Of course I did, you stupid girl." He chuckles sardonically.

"Hey. You can leave if you're going to talk to me like that. I don't need to take your bullshit anymore." My hand drops from the pendant, and I fuel myself with the fire of my rebirth. "You came to me, not the other way around. So, the way I see it, you can crawl back from whatever hole you left because I don't want you here."

"Well, well, well. Look who finally grew a spine.

Maybe you learned something from me after all." A smug look of satisfaction creeps onto his face and I want nothing more than to knock it right-the-fuck-off. But he's right. His wounds were part of the hurt I've had to overcome, turning me into the stronger woman I am today.

"Yes. Thank you, *father*. For teaching me that your being such a piece of shit has absolutely nothing to do with me. That your being worthless has nothing to do with me. That when you called me all those names, treated me like garbage, that it was just *you* projecting your own feelings onto me." I take a step forward, poking the tall lanky man in the chest. "So, yes. Thank you. Thank you for being such a garbage human being that I had no choice but to overcome all of the shit you left behind."

Surprise registers on his face, but it's short-lived and quickly replaced by furious rage. "You stupid bitch!"

My father moves so fast, I don't see it, his fist flying at my head with full speed and force.

I don't get to respond because in one instant, my world spins. But even as my body crumples to the ground and as the walls around me close, I know that I lived. Just for me, and that is enough to carry me through the darkness that covers me with its cold blanket of indifference.

It is enough, because I have truly lived. If only for a moment.

HUNTER

"Are you sure they've got our lines tapped?" I question my brother for what feels like the millionth time.

It's been three weeks since I've talked to my girl, but the thought of someone attacking her because of me keeps me from calling. I can't jeopardize her safety out of a selfish need. *I won't.*

"Yes. Like I've already said, our phone lines are compromised. No matter how many times we scramble them, there's a breach. It's almost as if we had a mole on the inside, sabotaging our every move." Jack rubs at his temples, a long frustrated sigh leaving his lips.

You and me both, brother. You and me both.

"If it seems like there's a mole, then there's a mole. What about your head of security? Armando, is it?" Matt turns toward Jace whose face is turning a bright shade of red.

All of the Crown brothers are in Miami, each one of us occupying a room at Jace's beach house.

"Don't go there. He's like another brother to me." Jace's eyes drift to the door where the man in question is standing guard.

Over the past few weeks we've gotten to know Armando, and I can safely say that he's good people. "I've got a good read on him. He isn't the mole."

"Then who is?" Austin's green eyes land on me, and despite the vast secrets I hold, this just isn't one of them.

"I've got no clue. Maybe—" I don't get to finish my

sentence because my phone is ringing and the number that pops up sends warmth running through me.

My girl. I've memorized the digits to the bunker's line but have never dared dial them. Yet here she is, my beautiful baby doll, reaching out to me again, even after the shit way I treated her last night.

God, never in my life have I felt like such a crap human, intentionally hurting the girl I love. But I had to. There was no other choice.

The line rings for the fifth time before it dies, but almost immediately, Jack's phone starts up.

"Hello?" Jack scowls two seconds upon answering, letting me know something isn't right. "Ericson, slow down. I can't understand you."

My former friend's name coming out of Jack's mouth isn't what I expected to hear, the act alone bringing me to my feet as I close the distance between us.

"Right. Okay." There's a pause that drains years from my life. "I'll let him know." Jack ends the line, his eyes drifting up to mine as he pockets his cell. "That was Ericson. There's been an incident with his father and Melissa."

Oh, fuck no. I'm going to kill him. I'm going to kill that motherfucker.

Trying to calm my breathing, I close my eyes and suck in a lungful of air. "Where's Mel?"

"She's in stable condition, but she was beat pretty bad." My knees rattle and I feel myself about to drop.

I wasn't there. I didn't protect her. I couldn't keep her safe.

My world has gone to shit, the ache inside too much to bear. But as my brother stands, placing a hand on my shoulder, it's then that his words suck the life right out of me. "I'm sorry, Hunter, but the baby didn't make it."

The baby. *The baby.* I didn't even know there was a baby. But as my mind flits back to the cabin where I first took her, there was nothing that separated us, nothing that stopped my seed from taking hold and claiming its rightful place—deep inside my baby's womb.

Each and every time I took her, it was without protection. Something I never do, but with her, it didn't even cross my mind. The need to be so close to her with absolutely nothing between us was so ingrained in my desire that it wasn't even an afterthought.

"Hunter." Jack's hands are on either shoulder, shaking me back into the here and now. "Snap-the-fuck-out, brother. Your girl needs you."

He's right, and the longer I stand here in this daze of self-deprecating pity, the longer she's alone. That just won't do.

I'm coming, baby doll. Daddy's on his way.

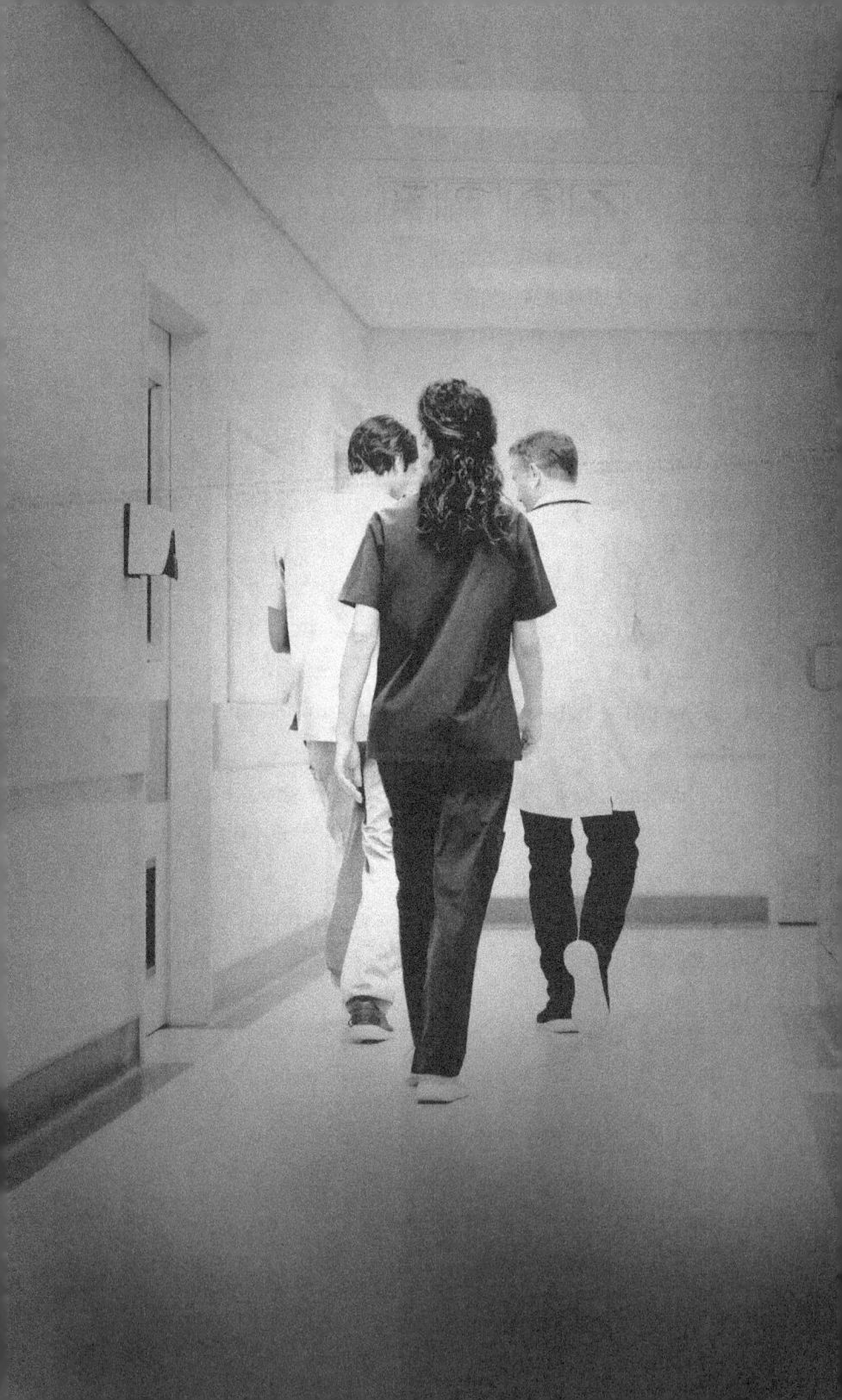

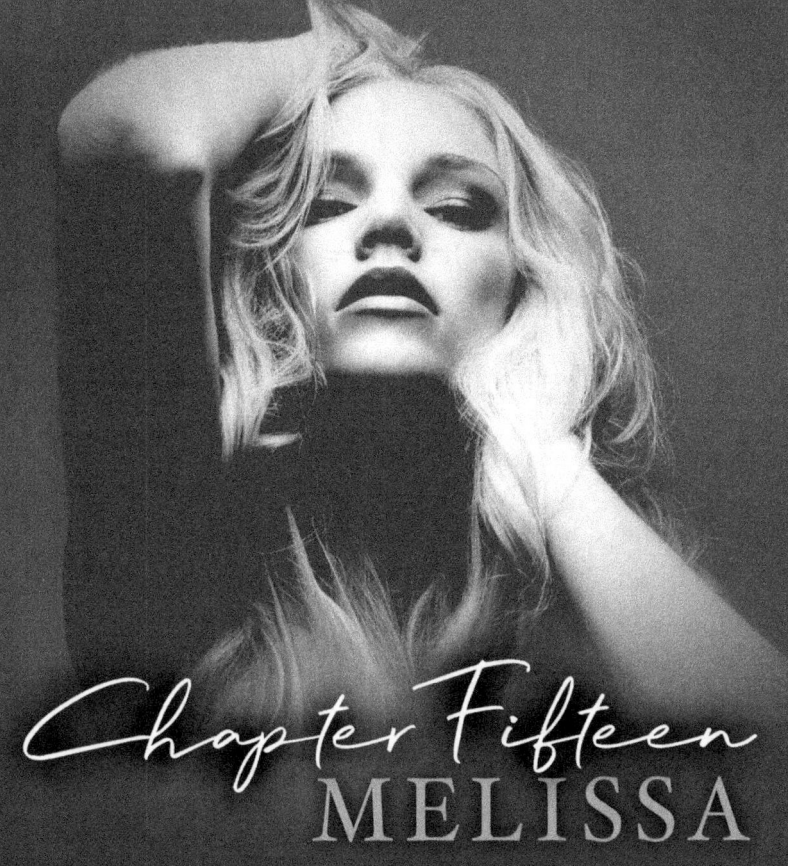

Chapter Fifteen
MELISSA

Tears stream down my face as my hands desperately cling to my abdomen. *Our baby. I was growing our baby.*

Never will I get to see its tiny face or count its tiny little fingers or toes. *Gone. Our baby is gone.*

And if the pain couldn't get any more gut wrenching, the door creaks open, the other half of my soul stepping right through it.

Fury. It's all there is. Nothing but boiling rage consumes me and all I see is red.

"Get out! Get the fuck out!" My vocal cords rattle as

my hands fling to either side of me, gripping onto the bed rails for dear life. "Right now! Leave!"

The tears that'd already been falling down my face intensify, my vision blurring and going right along with them.

"Baby doll." Hunter walks toward me with speed, his massive frame crawling onto the bed as he covers my body with his own. "God, I'm so sorry, baby. So damn sorry." His arms have flung around me, pulling me closer into him as his head falls to the crook of my neck, both hands holding me tight. "I'm so damn sorry."

I lose it. I break down and lose all strength I'd had, turning into a pile of mush in this man's arms. There's no more exchange of words. Tears are the only communication between us, both mine and his.

Hunter shakes against me, his own sadness dripping down my back as we both grieve the loss of what will never be.

It's these moments in life that make absolutely no sense. *What lesson was I supposed to learn? Why did a life who'd just begun lose its spark?*

I don't know. Have no damn clue. All I know is that this shared sadness stretches for what feels like forever before there's a clearing of someone's throat.

"Glad you could finally make it." There's a hint of sarcasm behind my brother's tone and it's not something Hunter takes lightly.

With uncanny speed, the large man removes himself

from my bed, only to come toe-to-toe with Eric, their faces a mere breath apart. "Watch your mouth, Ericson. This is all your fault."

My brother scoffs, taking a good step back. "My fault? Last I checked, I wasn't the one that got her pregnant."

This makes Hunter turn an almost purple shade of red. "Are you fucking kidding me? I thought I told you—*No visitors*! What in the hell made you think your dead-beat father was the exception?!" He shoves at Eric, my brother taking a tumble into the wall before he's righting himself, his palms up in defense.

"Hey, he said he needed to talk to me. Said he wasn't going to be stopping by the bunker until later that day." His brows have dropped, and the pain etched on his face isn't something I miss.

My brother has his own set of demons, and I don't doubt him for a second. I know he didn't mean any harm by it. Was probably looking forward to Bruce's fatherly attention—something that was rare in our home—but Hunter isn't buying it.

"I don't give a damn what that man told you. He's a known liar and cheat. What makes you think he'd suddenly have good intentions?" Thankfully, Hunter doesn't make another move against Eric, he simply stands there with both hands on his hips, his head shaking in disapproval.

"I fucked up." Eric's eyes close before he's running the palm of his hand over his face.

"Yeah, you did." Hunter gives my brother his back,

his eyes landing on me, the honey-colored orbs trailing my body from head to toe. "Mel is coming home with me."

"What?! Like hell I am!" I may be torn into a million pieces but there is no way I'm shacking up with Hunter.

He's my kryptonite and I've just now started to overcome the shellshock of our last conversation.

"He's right, Mel. I can't keep you safe." Eric chimes in, his sheepish expression one I'm not used to. "Just look at you."

My brother's eyes trail my battered body, most of which I had no memory of happening. Bruce's first punch pretty much knocked me out, with only bits and pieces of his beating filtering through my consciousness.

Turning toward Hunter, I see that his jaw is ticking, eyes narrowed on Eric.

"I don't care. I'm not going with him." I steel my face, knowing myself well, and if I'm left alone with this man, I'm bound to shatter once more.

Hunter lets out a deep breath, his eyes closing as his chest rises and then falls. "Ericson, can you give me a minute with your sister?"

My brother looks between us, his eyes flitting to Hunter and then back to mine. "Okay, but I'm just outside this door. You holler at me if you need me, Mel."

My heart warms. Eric and I don't have the best of relationships, but it's good to know that he's here when it really matters.

Nodding, I answer, "Thank you. And Hunter, you have ten minutes... starting now."

I look at the clock, intent on keeping my word. I'm not sure how much more of him I can take.

"I didn't mean it. Any of it." Hunter's words have my eyes abandoning their post and fully taking his features in. "Our lines were being tapped. They were listening to everything we were saying and I couldn't risk them finding out what you meant to me."

I'm stunned speechless. Not sure how to feel about what he's just said.

"Mel," Hunter lowers one of the bed rails, his large frame lowering down to the edge as he grabs hold of my hand. "My family isn't perfect. Far from it. We've got secrets that run deep. Battles that still rage on with *very* unsavory people."

My brows push together and nose scrunches. "I sort of figured that out when we had to go into hiding." I chuckle, but there's no humor in it. "And hey, turns out I didn't need protecting from your family. Just my own."

"Baby..." Hunter shakes his head, his glistening eyes trailing my body once more. "That should've never happened. If I'd kept you with me, this... our baby..."

I break down. I can't help it. Tears start falling and my body shakes from the godawful sobs that are wrenched right from my chest.

"Shhh, baby." Hunter pulls me onto his lap, one of his large palms rubbing slow circles on my back. He doesn't bother telling me it's going to be okay, because we both know, it never will be.

There will always be this part of us missing, forever lost.

"From now on, I'll keep you safe. From both my family and yours. You have my word."

A snot bubble forms and I wipe it against his shirt. "Fine, but that's what you get."

Hunter chuckles, "Baby, you could be covered in snot, and I'd still find you the sexiest woman on earth."

Unable to keep it in, I laugh, my cheeks smarting at the unusual sensation. "So, what now?"

"Now? We wait for the doctor to give you the all clear. Then we'll head back to the bunker, get your things and head home."

My body shudders in Hunter's embrace. "I can't go back there. I'm sorry."

Hunter nods, his face solemn. "No worries, baby. We'll figure it out." He lowers me down onto the bed, his lips finding my forehead and pressing a lingering kiss before he's standing upright. "But first, we need to get you out of here."

He walks over to the door, pulling it open only to find my brother's ear pressed against it.

"Hey!" Eric practically falls into the room from the door no longer holding him up.

"Were you eavesdropping?!" I'm screeching from my spot on the bed while Hunter just shakes his head.

"I was just trying to make sure you were okay." Eric's brows raise as he skirts around Hunter.

"Whatever, brother. I'm going to find the doc. You keep your eyes on my girl, and don't you take them off her for a second, you hear me?"

Eric rolls his eyes. "As if I would. I already feel guilty enough."

"Good," Hunter grunts before he's shutting the door behind him.

And as soon as he's gone, the energy shifts and my heart settles. Truth be told, I'm not sure how I'll manage being in close quarters with him after everything we've been through. Yes, there might be some logic behind the way he treated me, but it still doesn't shake the feelings he left behind.

"Girl! What happened to you?!" Hayley, the shop owner and high-school friend whisper-hisses, before her eyes float over my shoulder and toward Hunter. "Do you need me to call the Sheriff?"

Laughing, I place a hand on my friend's shoulder. "I know I look scary, but Hunter didn't do this. Bruce did."

Hayley sucks in a sharp breath. "That bastard. I knew he was always no good, but I didn't think he'd ever hurt his own daughter."

I scoff. "Well, looks like we were both wrong."

Cutting into the moment, Hunter clears his throat behind me, "We came to get some things for Mel. You do have things in her size, right?"

It took me some convincing, letting him know that Hayley's store would carry what I like. Yes, we could've driven an hour or two out into the big city, but there's something about supporting locals that's just a million times better.

"Of course, I do. She's my best customer." Hayley laughs as she walks over to the new arrivals. "Get your butt over here, girl. I've got to show you what I just got in."

"You don't have to tell me twice!" I'm fixin' to be in hog heaven when the bell over the door chimes.

"There you are. I've been looking for you everywhere." Matt's voice booms from behind me, but it's Hayley's expression that has my rapt attention.

My friend is like a deer in headlights. *Interesting.*

"I told you. I needed to get my girl some things." The way Hunter so casually calls me his girl almost makes me swoon, but if I were being honest with myself, my heart is still leery after that phone call.

"Yeah, well, I thought you would make like every other normal person and head into the city." Matt is chuckling but his face freezes as soon as his eyes land on Hayley.

Very interesting.

"Normal is overrated." Hayley glares at him, her hands instantly flying to her hips. "I'll have you know that I carry pieces that even the big city can't get their hands on."

"She has a point. I know. I've tried." I'm nodding along with my friend, but the wheels in my head are turning. "Do you two know each other?"

"Yes." "No." Are uttered simultaneously with Hayley being the one in denial.

Matt rolls in his lips, but just nods. "My bad. I must've mistaken you for someone else."

Hayley looks him dead in the face, one brow arched. "*Mhm*. Must've."

Needing to end the awkward stare off, I clap my hands together. "Alrighty then. Hayley, how about we let these two catch up and you can show me the goods."

My friend slaps on a fake smile if I ever saw one. "Right. In fact, there's a new shipment out back. Why don't I show you?"

Nodding, I follow her toward the stockroom and away from the Crown brothers. We might've put distance between us but it's obvious one of them is still on her mind.

"Care to tell me what that was about?" I raise a brow as she goes to open a box.

"Nope." She doesn't even look at me as she answers.

"Okay, but I'm here if you ever need to vent. I know just how frustrating those Crown men can be."

She laughs at this. "Yeah. Well thank you, but I have nothing to say."

I roll in my lips and nod. She may deny it all she wants, but there's definitely more to this story, and as all things, it's only a matter of time before it's out.

Chapter Sixteen
HUNTER

"Did you find Bruce?" I press Matt for answers, needing that motherfucker six-feet under as soon as possible.

"Nah. His trail dies out halfway down the mountain. It's like he disappeared into thin air." Matt rubs at his jaw, his brows furrowed in deep thought.

"Part of this lands on Ericson. He didn't tell anyone about the bunker's rear exit." My jaw ticks, knowing that my friend fucked up more than once.

"I get not wanting to show all your cards, but damn, they were on lockdown. Who'd have thought that their threat would come from within their own family, not ours." Matt chuckles, but there's no humor in it. "Did Ericson ever figure out what Bruce wanted in the first place?"

"Money. Isn't that what's behind most bullshit anyway? Apparently, it wasn't the first time Bruce had raided his house, looking for things to pawn."

Matt's brows raise, his hand running through his hair as he whistles. "Shit, he did a lot more than taking things to pawn."

"Yes. He did." I count to five in my head, trying to calm the demons that threaten to take over. "And as soon as I find him, he'll pay for that."

"Well, it might have to take the back burner. There's been some developments down in Mexico. *El Jefe's* brother has gone missing."

"When did this happen?" I'm taken aback by this news. I've had eyes on the Cardenas' compound since *El Jefe* and his brother were taken in as prisoners. None of my alerts had gone off.

"That's why I came to find you. You left this behind in Florida." He hands me one of my tablets. The one that's directly linked to Raul's cell.

Shit. If I thought Mel's safety was important before, it blows everything else out of the water now. Raul is known for his ruthless acts of violence, and he knows full well what our family is hiding.

"Do the other brothers know yet?"

Matt raises a brow, his gaze assessing. "No. I figured

this was something you wanted to keep to yourself, otherwise you would've told us about the miniature surveillance hub you've got going on."

I smirk. "You're right. Let's just say there's stuff I'm holding onto, and when it gets out, you won't want to be anywhere near it."

Matt's head jerks back in surprise. "You know I'm here if you need to share the weight, brother. It isn't fair for you to carry that burden all on your own."

I nod, appreciating the gesture but not planning to take him up on it. There's only one other Crown brother that knows the truth, and that's Jace.

Our father trusted him with *El Jefe's* will. The will that lists Austin Crown as his sole heir. That's a can of worms I prefer not to go down unless it's absolutely necessary.

"Thanks, Matt. I appreciate it, but for now, how about you just help me find Bruce? I'll worry about Raul."

My brother's brows hit his hairline. "You aren't planning on going after him all on your own, are you?"

I scoff. "Fuck no. I've got Mel to protect." But I do plan on pulling in Jace and his men. He's the one with the will, and there's no doubt that he will be Raul's first target.

"Soooo, how are you going to go after Raul?"

"Don't you worry about that. Just get back to Florida. I have a feeling things are about to get hectic down there."

Matt shakes his head before turning around and heading toward the door. "Fine, brother. I don't know what you've got planned, but this shit feels like it's about to bite you in the ass."

"God, I hope you're wrong," I mumble under my breath as Matt clears the threshold, the bell chiming once more overhead.

There are only two things that have the power to bring me down—something happening to Mel, and Austin finding out who his biological father is. Both have the power to rock me to my core. The first because Melissa is my world, and the second... well, it unleashes Pandora's box.

Melissa

"Just how many properties do you own?" I'm staring at the expansive windows overlooking Lake Opalaka in this stunning cabin.

This place is unlike my own tiny house or where we first made love. It's huge, with a u-shaped sectional overlooking the lake and a massive chef's kitchen to the right.

"A few." Hunter is so nonchalant about this it makes me chuckle.

"Just a few." I shake my head as I let my hand trail over the granite countertops before heading straight for the fridge and pulling it open. "Is this where you live? It's fully stocked."

Hunter shakes his head. "No, I live further up the ridge."

As he's talking I notice that not only is the fridge stocked, but it's stocked with all of my favorite things. "How… why?"

I'm at a loss for words, yet again. Yes, I'm still leery of his intentions—that phone call still lingering in the back of my mind—but damn, does he have a way of making me feel special, right before he's tearing me back down.

I guess that's what I'm expecting. Waiting for the other shoe to drop, because if history has taught me anything, it's only a matter of time.

Right on cue, strong arms wrap around me from behind as Hunter lowers his lips to the crook of my neck. "I told you, baby doll. I know everything about you."

A shiver runs through me before I get it together and give him some sass. "You know, some might say that's a little creepy."

Hunter laughs. "I don't give a shit what some might say. I only care about what you have to say."

"Well, I have a lot to say, and I'm not sure you're going to like it."

Hunter quickly turns me around, his eyes searching mine before he's lifting me up and seating me on the counter. It's too much too soon and the motion makes me wince, my body still sore from the beating.

Hunter takes note, his face contorting as he takes a step

back. "Fuck, baby. I'm so sorry. I should've been watching. I should've kept you by my side."

"But you didn't. You pawned me off on my brother and then treated me like shit when you called."

Hunter rolls in his lips and nods. "I see you're still upset about that."

I scoff. "Of course I'm still upset about that! I get why you said you did it, but it doesn't change the fact that it destroyed me when you did."

A pained look takes over his masculine features and my chest squeezes. How can I hurt for this man when I'm still licking my own wounds? *Because you love him.*

"I know it hurt you, baby, but if it meant keeping you safe, then it had to be done. I won't ever regret doing something that was in your best interest." His brows drop and his eyes search mine, trying to convey his truth, but I just don't want to hear it.

"No. I don't want that. I want you to trust me with the truth, no matter how painful or how dangerous. I'm a big girl and you can't keep me safe from the world." I look past him and out the window, a lone tear trailing down my face. "Look at what happened in the bunker. You did everything you could to keep me safe, even hurt my heart in the process, but in the end—it wasn't enough."

Hunter sucks in a sharp breath, and it's then I realize how this all sounded. Needing to rectify my wrongs, I cradle his sharp jawline in my hands, the thick stubble scraping against my palms and making them itch to touch more. "Hey... This wasn't your fault, so don't you think that for a second. I'm not blaming you. I'm just saying that no matter what you do, you can't control every single thing that happens around me."

Hunter scoffs. "Fuck if I don't try."

I'm shaking my head when Hunter presses his forehead to mine, the tender act making my heart swoon.

Wrapping my legs around his waist, I press myself closer, needing to feel his body on mine. "Promise me, Daddy. If you want this to work, then you have to give me nothing but the truth—even when you think I can't handle it."

"Baby, you know I can't deny you when you ask me so sweetly." Hunter rolls his hips, and it's then I feel the thick bulge pressing against my slit.

"Mmmph, that feels so good." I grind against him, making sure to let the top of his massive length nudge my clit and make me groan. "Doesn't Daddy want to slide inside his girl's tight little cunt?"

"*Fuuuuuck*, Mel. Don't talk to me like that or I'll be forced to push you down on this counter and rut into you, making that wet little snatch drain every last bit of my cum."

"Well, if you want to play, then you have to promise." I'm raising a brow while trailing a finger down his chest, my fingers wrapping around his impressive girth.

"*Baby*," Hunter hisses, but his next actions surprise me. He's taking my hand and removing it from his body. "In all seriousness, as much as I'd love to be balls deep in you, you have to know that I can't give you what you want."

My mouth drops open in disbelief. He's rejecting me. *Again.*

"Are you kidding me right now?" I scooch to the side before dropping to the ground with a wince. "All I'm asking for is honesty, and you can't even give me that?"

Hunter sighs, his head dropping back before he answers. "Not if it means costing you your safety." His head falls forward as his eyes seer into mine. "Not tasting you, not feeling your walls grip around me... that's a sacrifice I'm willing to make if it means I'm keeping you alive."

"But it's not only your choice to make!" I'm shouting at the top of my lungs, trying to make this man understand, but it doesn't seem like I'll be getting through.

"It is when I'm the one holding the information, baby doll."

"No! Don't you 'baby doll' me." I take a step back, pacing in front of the massive windows, needing to get my head on straight. "*This.* I knew *this* would happen."

"What?" Hunter's brows push together and his nose scrunches, the act making him almost look childlike. *Oh, but I know better.*

He's just like *them.*

"You followed me around all this time, luring me into this false sense of safety. *He really cares. He must really love me.* No, I never thought you loved me as more than an honorary little sister, but I at least thought you truly cared."

I throw my hands up in the air, a deranged laugh falling from my lips. "How stupid was I? Believing in intentions that I had conjured all on my own. You never once told me you loved me or that you cared. Not once. Yet here I was, creating all of these make-believe scenarios in my head where one day, you'd finally see. See that you love me. That you need me as much as I need you."

Hunter takes a step forward but I shoot my hand up, palm exposed. "But, baby doll, I *do* care."

"No. Enough with this baby doll bullshit. All I've ever asked for is honesty. That's it. And you couldn't even give me that. If you truly cared this wouldn't even be a thing, you'd just agree to it, and we'd move on. We'd be upstairs, fucking—*good and hard*—before making sweet love."

Hunter's body shudders at my words and I see how much he'd like that. *Well, too bad.* He doesn't get access anymore. Never again will I trust him with that part of me.

"Melissa. I see what you're saying, but you need to know that I love you enough to give up that part of us if it means I'm keeping you safe." He takes two steps forward, his hands landing on either bicep before his fingers dig in deep. "You need to see that, baby. This is for you. All for you. You are my world, and if anything were to happen to you, I'd die. There'd be no point to keep going. You'd take every bit of joy and suck it right out of this life because you're what makes it worth living."

My lip wobbles and vision blurs, but I refuse to give into my heart and his pretty words. "And I see what you're saying, but that isn't love. *That's control.* You want to control the situation, uncaring of what impact it has on my heart. What good is my living in this world if the life I lead is a miserable one?"

This makes him blink, his jaw set and cheek twitch. "Mel—"

A cell phone rings off in the distance and the moment is broken. Just when I thought I'd gotten through to him, life intervenes once more.

"I have to take that. It's my brother's ringtone." Hunter drops his hold on my body and it's a miracle I don't crumple to the ground as he turns.

If ever there were a sign that we aren't meant to be, this is it. No matter how hard I try, how hard I push, Hunter Crown will never truly be mine.

Chapter Seventeen
HUNTER

"This better be important, or so help me—"

"Whoa, what's going on?" Matt's voice trickles through the line.

"Nothing. Just tell me why you called."

"As a matter of fact, it is important. Remember how we found out Raul had escaped?"

"Yeah?" The hairs on the back of my neck stand at attention and I know whatever he says next isn't going to be good.

"Well, Mila has gone missing and we think it's Raul."

"What the fuck? When did this happen?" My heart is

beating overtime, wondering if the fucker has another connection on the way to Colorado.

"Just now. Her detail had followed her to a doctor's appointment... get this... we think Mila might be pregnant."

I shake my head, blowing out a long breath. "Jesus, how is Jace taking all of this?"

"How do you think? Not well. With all of your surveillance, do you have any clue what they'd be after?"

"Yeah, and if they're wanting to trade Mila for it, I bet Jace might just give it to them."

"Wait... so Jace knows too?! I thought we were womb buddies. Does that not mean anything to you?" It might seem like Matt is making light of this, but I hear the hurt in his voice.

"It isn't like that, brother. Dad gave him the will first, I only happened to find out when I'd been trailing the girls."

Matt hisses. "Okay, you're going to have to tell me everything."

Resigning myself to the fact that it's time I let my brothers in, I walk over to the study and shut the door behind me, making sure Mel isn't within earshot. This information, like I said, has the power to unleash Pandora's box and I'm not ready for that confrontation just yet.

"It's about Austin and his bio dad. Are you sitting down?" I pause waiting for Matt to confirm. "Okay. It's *El Jefe*. Turns out he has a slew of bastard children running about but Austin was his firstborn. His will leaves the entire Cartel's fortune to him. The land, the money, the gold. Everything."

"*Holyfuckingshit.*"

"Yeah. That's an understatement. And to make matters worse, Raul is of the mindset that all that fortune belongs to him. He made that clear when he murdered his brother in hopes of getting his hands on the will and everything that came along with it."

"This is some insane shit. So how did you find out about the will and how does Raul know that Jace has it?" There's a door shutting in the background and the creaking of a chair as Matt sits down.

"I thought you said you were sitting down." I'm shaking my head at the little shit.

"Man, no way in hell I thought it was going to be this crazy. Go on. Tell me how Raul knew."

"Process of Elimination. He'd been working alongside our father for decades. Originally, he thought it'd be Austin himself, but it became clear he didn't have the will after their abduction in Mexico."

"And? How does that equate to Jace having what he wants?" Matt presses for what I've been asking myself all along.

"Next in line would be one of us, but why he chose Jace is still a mystery. The only thing I can think of is the stuff I've dug up on Mila's mother, Catherine. She used to date the attorney who laundered for *El Jefe*. That's quite the coincidence if you ask me."

"I'd say so. Do you think Catherine was sent to dig up information? Maybe look for the will herself?"

I'm about to answer when there's a beep, another call wanting to connect. Looking down, I see that it's the number to Jace's beach house. "Hold on Matt, I'm going to patch Jace in."

"Okay."

A few seconds pass before our brother's voice is crackling through the receiver. "Hunter, you there?"

"Yeah, brother. So is Matt. We're both on the call."

"Okay, good. You'll never believe the shit that just went down." Jace is talking a mile-a-minute, but I wouldn't expect any different with Mila having gone missing. "It's Catherine, she's the mole. She's the one who's been sabotaging the calls."

"Fuck, I knew it!" I exclaim and the line goes silent.

Two beats pass before Jace's eerily calm voice comes through. "What do you mean you knew?"

"I knew that she'd dated Mila's dad, the attorney who laundered money for *El Jefe*. I suspected that her getting pregnant with your baby was just a ploy to get closer to you and find the will."

"And you didn't think to fucking tell me that!?" Jace is screaming into the line, the pitch so intense I have to pull the cell away from my head. "What the fuck Hunter?"

"I wasn't sure. I didn't want to give you half-assed information." I'm shrugging, even though I know they can't see me.

"Well, she isn't pregnant. That was all a lie. And get this…"

"Go on, spit it out!" Matt shouts from his end.

"That attorney? He isn't Mila's dad, *El Jefe* is," Jace adds to all of our surprise.

"Get-the-fuck-out-of-here. This is some real Jerry Springer shit!" Matt chuckles into the line, but it isn't really funny.

"Yeah. And there's more… Catherine isn't Mila's mom. She's her sister!"

I hear something slam on someone's end and I can't help but ask, "Everyone okay?"

"Yes." Both brothers answer but it's Jace who elaborates. "Hunter, she wants the will for herself and the attorney, but I'll be damned if I give it to them."

"Good. Don't. We'll find Mila, brother. I promise." I send Jace my assurances, but even as I do, I'm not sure I'll be able to deliver.

"So, hold up. Catherine has no connection to *El Jefe's* brother then? Raul?" Matt asks something that had slipped past both Jace and me.

"Besides being a part of that twisted family tree? Nope. She's only working with the attorney, John McComb."

"Fuck, so not only do we have to work on a rescue mission for Mila, but we also have to be on guard of Raul —a psychopath who also wants to get his hands on the will." I can hear Matt pacing, his Italian loafers clicking on his marble floor.

"Seems that way," I answer, though it isn't really needed. We all know what's at risk.

"Alright. Now that we have all that out in the open, what's the plan and when are we telling Austin? This is bound to get out and when he figures that we knew all along, he's going to be pissed, if not just hurt." Jace voices something that we'd both been thinking about for some time now. It's quite the secret to keep, and my only hope is that this doesn't destroy our bond.

"We do what we can to find Mila, all without giving those fuckers what they want…And as for Austin? I guess we'll cross that bridge when we get to it." A lump forms in my throat, knowing that this is a lose-lose situation and the best we could hope for is minimal damage.

"That sounds like a shit plan with respect to Austin. You sure we shouldn't just come out and tell him?" Matt seems hesitant and I can see why, so far, it's just me and Jace who have carried this burden, but now, he's technically in on it too.

"I think he's right, Hunter. We should tell him before the rescue," Jace adds, and I can hear the anxiety in his voice. He has a lot on the line.

"You guys aren't thinking straight. How do you think he'll react if we tell him before the mission? He won't go into it thinking clearly and that's a recipe for disaster. He needs to be sharp and lacking any emotional turmoil." This is the basics and something they would remember if they weren't basing their decisions on emotions instead of logic.

"Fine, but I want to make it clear that I was against this every step of the way." Matt adds, trying to wash his hands of this secret.

"Oh, don't worry little brother. I'll take the heat for it when it comes down to it."

"Um, excuse me. I'm only younger than you by like five minutes."

"Hey, that's still five minutes your elder," I counter.

"If you two are done with your bickering, I'm going to get with the team and let them know of our plan. How soon can you get down here?"

"I'm on my way," Matt chimes in.

"I need to get Mel ready, but we'll be there in a couple of hours. I doubt she'll want to stay behind for this."

Jace sucks in a sharp breath. "Yeah, I'm just wondering how that dynamic will play out with our prisoner. You know how Catherine and her get on. Now with all of this, we'll definitely need to keep them separated."

"You don't need to tell me twice. My girl is quite the spitfire. There's no doubt she'd be clawing her face off upon arrival."

My brothers chuckle, but I'm not joking. Mel is fiercely loyal to those she loves, and as I hang up the line, I pray that I'm still on that very short list.

"We're leaving." I shout up to the loft where Mel has parked herself to pout.

"I'm not going anywhere." Her bellow comes out sounding muffled, making me think she's been crying.

Jesus. That's my fucking weakness.

"Baby doll, we need to go to Florida. It's about Mila."

I hear rustling, and before I know it, my girl is scurrying down the ladder. "Why didn't you say so! Is she okay? Tell me she's okay!"

I blow out a breath, trying this honesty crap even though I know it's going to hurt her. "She's missing."

Mel's mouth drops open—and call me a sick bastard, but the site just begs for the taking.

"When? How? How can we get her back? Tell me we're getting her back. Please!" Her legs wobble and she starts to drop right before my very eyes.

"I got you, baby. Daddy's got you." Pulling her smaller frame into mine, I hold her close. "I promise you, we'll find her."

And right then, I vow to move heaven and hell to get that girl back. Not for Mila's sake, and hell, not even for Jace, but for my girl.

"Come on, doll. Let's get your bags and head to the airfield. We'll touch down in a couple of hours and I'll make good on my promise."

Mel is blinking up at me, her eyes glossing over as she nods. "You better my feral Buddha, or I'm taking you right over that cliff like I promised."

This stops me in my tracks. "And you better be joking, Mel."

My girl rolls her eyes. "Of course I'm joking. But that doesn't mean you're not still in the doghouse."

"Alright, baby doll. Whatever you say." I chuckle, even though the situation calls for anything but. "Whatever you say."

Chapter Eighteen
MELISSA

THIS IS MY FIRST TIME FLYING PRIVATE, AND TO SAY THAT it's nothing I could have imagined would be putting it mildly. *It's insane.*

The seats are the softest leather I've ever felt and the bathrooms? Who knew they had full bathrooms in these things? Not to mention there's a bedroom. The bedroom where Hunter has been holed up the last fifteen minutes.

He got a call and the look on his face as he moved to the back of the jet wasn't very comforting.

Just as I'm about to go knock on the door and see what's going on, it swings open, my broody man walking through it with a look that speaks of trepidation. *Oh god.* I brace myself for whatever is about to come out of his mouth.

"Baby doll…"

"Just give it to me. I can handle it."

Hunter sits next to me on the bench seating, his hand automatically going to my bouncing knee. "They've gotten a hold of Mila."

"That's great news!" I let out a breath I didn't know I was holding. I'm about to fling myself at him when I see the look on his face. "Oh no. There's more isn't there?"

He nods, his eyes squinting before they're glossing over. "Jace has been shot. We're not sure he's gonna make it."

My breathing stutters and a strangled noise is all I can muster. *But how?*

"Things got hairy in the retrieval. Jace didn't want to wait and went in without backup. Eventually his team caught up, but it was too late. McComb had taken him down."

"As in John McComb? Isn't that Mila's dad?"

Hunter gives me a pained smile. "About that, he isn't really her dad."

My mouth drops open. "What in the world?"

"And there's more than that, but I'll let Mila fill you in on it when she's ready."

This has my head cocking back "Wait… how long have you known this?" Hunter doesn't answer and that's all the response I need. "Wow, so you had this info on Mila's family all this time and you didn't care to fill her in?"

"Wasn't my place, baby doll."

"No. Don't you try to sweet talk your way out of this." I stand up and pace the center of the jet. "This is exactly what I meant about you being honest. You can't keep this shit from me."

Hunter's brows raise, the look of surprise one I don't understand.

"Look, Mel. When I found this out, we weren't exactly on talking terms besides a grunt of acknowledgement here and there."

"And after? What was your excuse then?" I cock my hip, my hand landing on my waist.

"After? Everything happened so fast I didn't have a chance to tell you." Hunter stands, his feet stopping right in front of mine. "But I'm telling you now." He places a kiss on my forehead. "And what's more, I promise to tell you everything I can, as long as it doesn't compromise your safety." Full lips press to the bridge of my nose. "I'll be your favorite news source. *Heard it here first.*"

And with that, Hunter presses a lingering kiss to my lips, his words mixed with the tenderness of this moment making me melt on the spot. I can't help it. I swoon, my foot kicking up and arms wrapping around my man. Because that's what he is, mine.

"Mr. Crown?" The stewardess calls. "We're beginning our descent. Is there anything else I could get you?"

And as my man swoops down for another kiss, he says the words that seal my heart, making it forever his. "No, ma'am. Got everything I need right here."

"HOLY SHIT. IS THIS WHERE MILA'S BEEN THE WHOLE time? The whole time I was in a literal hole underground, my best friend's been living it up in the lap of luxury?" I'm staring at the ocean from Jason's beachfront property as I hear Hunter chuckle from behind.

"No. Technically, she was in a penthouse."

This has me whirling around, my mouth falling open as my eyes practically bulge out. "Oh, hell no. I'm not high maintenance by any means but you owe me. Big time. If it were up to me, I would've been down here with my bestie, soaking up the vitamin D."

"The only vitamin D you'll be getting is from me. I'm locking you up in a bedroom and we aren't leaving for days." Hunter grabs me by the waist and pulls my body into his.

"Ha!" I'm pursing my lips to the side, biting back a smile. If ever I had to do a lockdown again, that's exactly how I'd want to spend it. But I'm not telling him that. "So, what now?"

"We wait for the helicopter to land. Thankfully, Jason is stable. He lost a lot of blood, but the doc thinks he should be waking up soon."

I breathe a sigh of relief, knowing that my best friend would be losing her shit if her man left this earthly plane. "How much longer till they get here?"

Just as Hunter goes to answer, there's a thudding sound from above, and looking up I see a helicopter descending on what must be a rooftop helipad—*because who doesn't have one of those?*

"Not much longer at all," Hunter answers, his hand dropping to mine as he pulls me inside. "Look, things might get a little messy and I might be gone for a while. Just giving you a heads up, there's some family business that needs to be handled and the next couple of hours are going to dictate how they go."

"What family business, and what can I do to help?" My brows push together as Hunter whirls me around, my body fitting so nicely into his as he cradles my face.

"God, have I told you how much I love you?" His expression is serious, his eyes so intense I don't know how to answer. I'm not used to this version of Hunter. Hell, I'm not used to this version of anyone. The only person who's ever told me they loved me is Mila.

"Nope. But you can tell me right after you tell me what you need from me." I raise a brow, wrapping both arms around him as my head cranes back. "Seriously, what's going on?"

His eyes narrow as his tongue pokes at the inside of his cheek. *This can't be good.* "I can't tell you."

Yup. It isn't good.

"Are you kidding me?" I try to pull back from his hold, but he hangs on tight. "Let me go!"

"No. I swear I have a good reason and you're just going to have to deal with it."

"I don't and I won't. I already gave you my terms." I give him one big shove and he finally releases me. "This is bullshit."

"Mel—" Hunter goes to reach for me but a clicking on the marble floor has us looking toward the hallway. There's an entourage of people surrounding a rolling bed, Jason Crown right smack dab in the middle with my best friend draped on top.

If ever there was a scene to snap me back down to reality, it's this. Life is so fragile and this moment is a reminder of that.

As if in slow motion, Mila whispers into Jason's ear, all while they're wheeled into a room. "Come back to us, please. The baby and I, we need you."

Like a magnet, my eyes are trained on Mila's hand as she takes Jason's and presses it to her abdomen before the stretcher comes to a complete stop—*just like my heart.*

My best friend is pregnant. Just like I would've been had I not lost our baby.

On instinct, my hand swings to the now empty womb, and the ache in my chest is one I just can't bear. It's a pain so deep it threatens to swallow me whole.

Right then, Hunter wraps his arms around me and presses his hands over mine. "Shhh, baby. It'll be okay."

This man, no matter how stubborn and difficult he might be, is always in sync with my pain. He always knows what pushes my buttons and brings to life the darkness I've long since battled.

But if that's the case, then why? Why can't he just give me what I need and be honest with me all the time? It isn't much to ask for, is it?

A flash of frustration hits me, the unbearable sensation making me itch to get out of Hunter's hold. He must sense it because he releases me, his eyes searching mine as soon as I've turned to face him.

"I think you need to leave me alone," I spit out before I've had time to really think this request through, but once it's out, I refuse to take it back.

"Like hell I will." Hunter pulls me into another room, having the frame of mind to keep this conversation away from the newly arrived couple. "Where's this coming from, Mel? Talk to me. Tell me why you're pushing me away."

I scoff. "I'm not pushing you away. I told you. If you want to be with me, then all I want is your honesty. Complete and brutal honesty at all times."

"Baby doll, it isn't that easy." His brows drop as he takes a step toward me, but I back away.

"Well, nothing worth having comes easy, does it?" I glare at him, refusing to give in, because I know that if I do, I'm only going to get hurt once more. "I'm staying until Mila tells me she doesn't need me. And until then, I need you to keep your distance. You can at least give me that, can't you?"

A beat passes as Hunter begins to pace, the sight making my heart stutter as I realize that I'll shatter if he actually does what I ask.

This is what I want, right? I'm keeping my heart safe. Safe from the man that's broken it time and time again.

But if this is for the best, then why do I already feel so broken?

I'm not left much time to ponder because my man is shoving me up against a wall, the feral look in his eyes speaking of nothing but hunger and rage.

"Baby doll, I'll never leave you alone. *Ever.* So don't ask it of me because it will be a resounding no each and every time." My mouth falls open, the veracity of his words visible in the rise and fall of his chest. And if my knees weren't already weak enough, Hunter trails a hand down my dress, only stopping to pull up the hem and slide his fat digits underneath my lace covered heat.

"God," I groan as he glides between my folds, feeling how undoubtedly turned on I am by his mere presence.

"Yes, doll. You can call me God because these fingers are the only thing you'll worship." He thrusts three inside, the sting of their fullness only dulled by his thumb pressing to my swollen clit. "And every time you try to push me away, I'll just have to work harder to remind you."

I'm mewling, liquid fire consuming my body as I writhe between the wall and his massive body. At this moment, I know it won't take much. The combination of his words and the possessive look in his eyes are enough to bring me to climax, reminding me that my body is and forever will be his.

"I'll do it as many times as it takes, baby, showing you that this tight little cunt belongs to me, and only me." Hunter bites down on my neck as he simultaneously rolls his thumb, pressing the pads of his fingers against my inner wall.

Holyfuckingshit. My legs shake and vision goes, nothing but black surrounds me.

Just then, Hunter growls against my heated flesh. "Fuck, baby. You make the prettiest sounds for Daddy."

He never slows his ministrations, dragging out my release for what feels like an eternity in this limbo of ecstasy. And as my body convulses in pleasure, I think this might just be the way I choose to go—in Hunter Crown's embrace.

Chapter Nineteen
HUNTER

There's so much I need to say but she isn't ready to hear it. I fear that if I say anything, she'll snap, fraying from the tattered nerves I myself have played a role in causing.

"Hunter, you're needed in the study," Matt bellows from the hallway, oblivious to the happenings of this room.

"This isn't over, Mel." I withdraw my fingers before licking them clean, raising a brow at the defiant look she throws me. *Such a spitfire, my girl.*

Mel rights herself, lowering her dress, but the dazed look on her face isn't something I miss.

Quickly clearing her throat, she looks toward the door. "It is, so you best get going. Looks like you have more secrets to discuss."

I scoff. *If only she knew.* These are things I would never wish on my worst enemies, let alone the woman I love.

Without saying another word, because there's nothing left to say, I step out of the room and toward the sound of shouting. *God.* It seems the day I've feared has finally arrived and it's time to face the music.

With unhurried steps, I cross the threshold to the study and take in the scene before me.

Austin is at Jack's throat, his fist balled up in his shirt. "You knew? You fucking knew, and you didn't tell me anything?"

Jack's eyes flit over Austin's shoulder and back to me. *Here goes nothing.*

"No, he didn't know. I did. Technically Jace and I, but he's already laid out, so if you're needing to take it out on anyone, take it out on me."

"Motherfucker!" Austin whirls, his feet sprinting to me before he throws a punch, the fist landing right against my jaw and sending my head flying back. "How could you? You! I thought you were my brother!"

Wiping the blood that's spilled from the corner of my mouth, I turn toward the man I will always consider kin, regardless of what a piece of paper says. "I am your brother, and that's why I wanted to protect you."

Austin's lip curls up in a snarl. "That isn't your fucking

job, Hunter. The moment you found out who my biological father was, you needed to tell me. It's my fucking life. It's my fucking choice."

Jesus, where have I heard this before? Maybe they're right and I've been wrong this entire time, trying to take on shit that doesn't belong to me just to keep those I love safe.

"There was no ill intent, brother. You have to know that."

Austin shakes his head, the look of disgust never leaving his features. "No. I don't. I don't have to know shit. The way I see it, you robbed me of that knowledge. All those years that I dug for information, all that time in Mexico." With these words he drops to his knees. "*Oh god. Blanca. If I'd known then what I know now, maybe Blanca would still be alive.*"

My stomach turns, knowing there's probably some truth to that. Despite that bitch being a two-timing whore, she didn't deserve to die the way she did.

Jack, always the voice of reason, steps in. "Hey, Austin. We don't know that. Fuck, we didn't even know that you'd been digging into the cartel in the first place. We all thought you were just having a family vacation, not going full vigilante on us."

"Exactly, that'd be like the pot calling the kettle black when it comes to keeping secrets," Matt chimes in.

"Ha!" Austin chokes out from his crouched position on the floor. "There's a huge fucking difference. Hunter's secret was about me. It was information on me." He turns to face me, his emerald eyes searing into mine with an intensity that has me looking away. "But my secret? I didn't even know what the fuck I was looking for. Could have been about all of us, or could have been nothing at all."

Jack, being the mediator he is, walks past me, stopping only once he's in front of Austin. "Hey, nobody could've predicted what was going to happen in Mexico. And just like we didn't know what you were up to, I'm sure Hunter had his reasons for keeping what he did to himself."

"There's no reason. No excuse." Austin shakes his head as his hands fling to his face in cover. "Fuck. Blanca. The kids. The poor kids."

"Blame me if you need to, but know that it was never my intention for anyone to get hurt." I take a couple of steps toward my brother, crouching down until I'm face to face with all of his sorrow. "Look, I wasn't sure if the information I had was accurate. There's no way I was going to drop such a big bomb on you without securing its veracity."

Austin scoffs as he stands, his six-foot-two towering over my still crouched position. "That's no excuse. You should have told me as soon as you found out, trusted me with that information and given me the choice to find out right along with you. But you robbed me of that. Robbed Blanca of a life she will never have. Robbed the kids of their own mother."

A tightness settles over my chest, the pressure threatening to squeeze out every drop of air in my lungs. *Maybe he's right. Maybe all those things are my fault.*

"No. You are no longer my brother. A brother wouldn't do what you did."

His last words haven't even registered before Austin is walking out of the study, the loud thud of the door slamming behind the only sound audible in the room.

Seconds tick by before I'm standing to my full height and Jack's hand is clapping against my back. "Give him some time, brother. He'll come around. Nobody could've predicted what happened with Blanca. And even if we could, there's no telling it wouldn't have happened regardless. She had her hand in all of this too."

I nod, but I'm not so sure. Austin's words sound so similar to those of my girl's. Maybe, just maybe, it's time I start letting people in. Stop carrying all of this bullshit on my own.

"Hate to break it to everyone, but this nightmare isn't over. Raul is still on the loose and we don't have a plan on how to deal with Catherine," Matt says as he pours three tumblers of whiskey before handing them out.

"Right. She doesn't know that her partner is dead." Jack takes the proffered rocks glass, before continuing. "I'd say we wait until Jace wakes up to make a decision as to Catherine, but we definitely need to move forward with locating Raul. Just because the lying bitch will no longer be looking for the will, it doesn't mean that *El Jefe's* brother won't."

"You're right. And until we get him into custody, then

none of us are safe." *Mel* isn't safe is what I really want to say.

"Fine. We'll get with the men of WRATH and see where they're at as far as his last known location. At least he's been spotted. That gives us something to go off of." Jack nods toward the door. "In the meantime, I think we just let Austin breathe. He's been given a lot of info that he needs to let sink in."

Matt snorts. "Yeah. Imagine finding out that your real dad is the notorious cartel leader who possibly offed your adopted father."

I growl, "Not '*possibly.*' There's no doubt in my mind that it was his men who ran our parents off the road."

Jack hums in agreement. "But that's neither here nor there now. We've got shit to do and dwelling on the past isn't going to fix it."

"Amen, brother. Amen." I nod before taking a substantial sip of Tortured Crown, needing the liquid fire to numb the pain of my mistakes. *If only it were that easy.*

But just like I'd thought before, there is no amount of booze that could bury the shitstorm my secrets have caused.

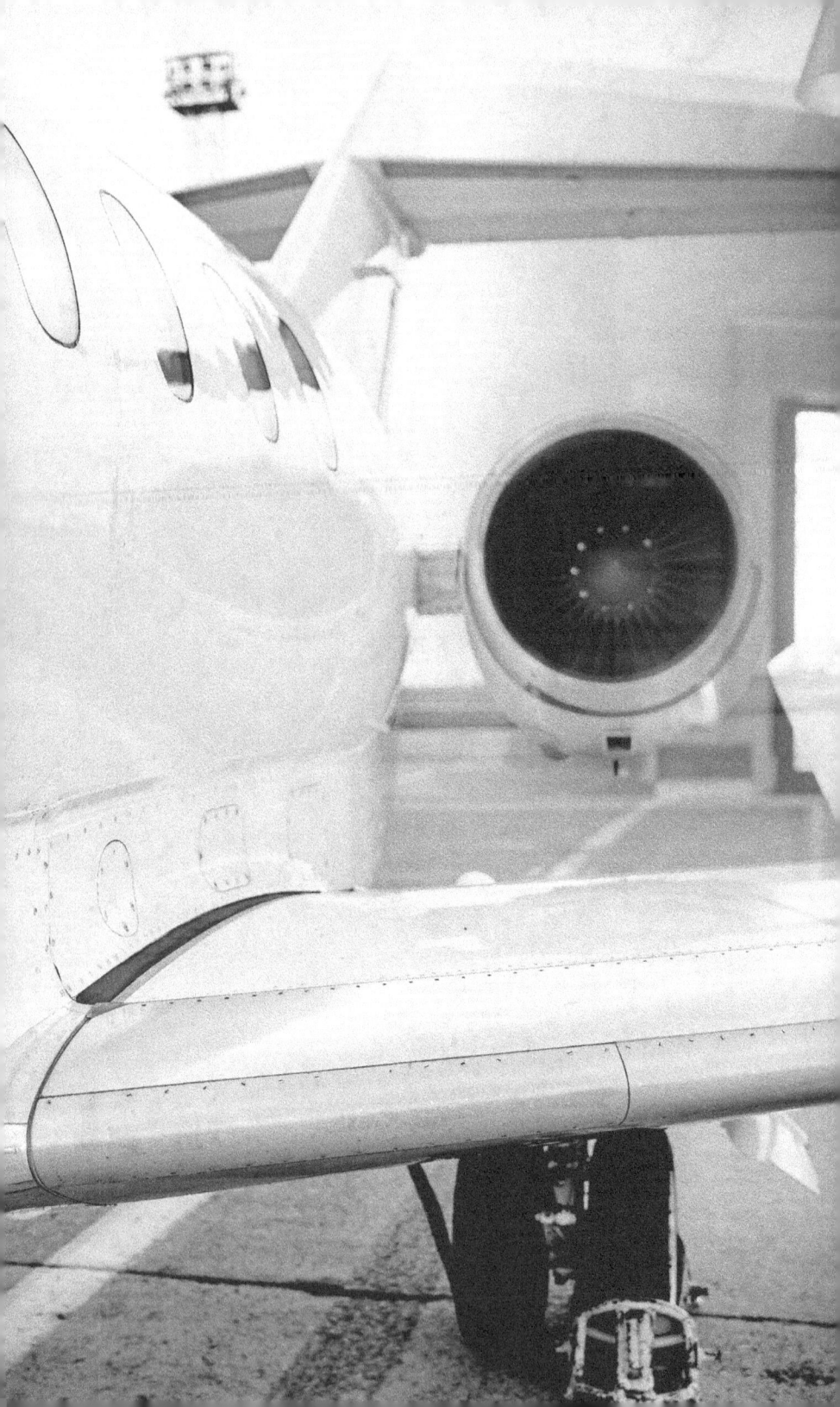

Chapter Twenty
MELISSA

"How are you holding up?" I hand Mila a cup of chamomile tea before I pour myself one.

It's been forty-eight hours since Jason fully woke up, the doc giving him the all clear. I mean, he can't go running a marathon, but he's no longer in danger of bleeding out by merely breathing.

"Me? I'm good, considering. What I want to know is how you're holding up." Mila peers over the lip of her cup as she takes a sip of her tea. "I swear you can feel the wall of ice as soon as you and Hunter are in the same room."

"Yeah, well… we sort of got into a fight…and then I

may have told him to stay away from me." I don't dare look at her as I take out the cream.

"Girl! Why on earth would you do that?! You're obsessed with him!" She's screeching so loud, I'm surprised everyone hasn't descended into the kitchen.

"Shhh! Be quiet!" I whisper-hiss. "It's a long story, but it's safe to say that my heart isn't open for any more heartache. And Hunter Crown? He's nothing but a world of hurt."

"Oh, Mel." There it is, the look of pity I'd been wanting to avoid and why I hadn't come clean to my best friend.

"No, don't look at me like that. I'm fine, really." I'm swirling the teaspoon in my cup when her words have me halting.

"Yeah, that's why you just poured tartar sauce into your tea."

Mouth hanging open, I inspect the bottle of *cream* I'd just taken out. Yup. Sure enough, it's fucking tartar sauce.

"You were saying?" Mila prompts.

"Whatever. I'm just a little absent-minded, that's all. You would be too if—"

"What?" Mila raises her brows as she puts her cup of tea down. "Spill it, girl. I know something's been weighing on you, I just don't know why you've been holding it back. You know we can tell each other anything, right?"

I sigh, placing the bottle of *not cream* back into the fridge. "I haven't wanted to offload on you because you've been going through a lot with Jason. For Christ's sake, he was on the brink of death."

She purses her lips to the side before she's patting the stool beside her. "Well, he isn't anymore, so dish."

Resigning myself to this gab session, my heart races as I take a seat and let her in on everything.

"Okay. Soooo, Hunter and I slept together before you left for Florida—"

"What!?" Mila screams and I instantly clap a hand over her mouth.

"Woman, you're going to have to be quiet if you want me to share." She nods against my hand and I slowly remove it, breaking the seal and letting the flood of whispered questions begin.

"I can't believe you didn't tell me." Mila whisper-shouts. "How many times? How many times have you been with him and hid it from me?"

My face tinges pink. "Depends on what you consider being 'a time.'"

"You little hussy, you." Mila gives me a little shove. "So, then what's the deal? Was he not any good? Does he have a small flinker?"

"Oh my god, Mila!"

"Now look who's being loud." She smirks, one lone brow raising. "Okay, so seriously. What happened?"

"He won't be honest with me. Not completely. Says that if it's not in my best interest, then he's going to keep it from me."

Mila's brows drop and one of her hands goes to mine. "Babe, that doesn't sound too bad."

"It is when his omissions have the power to break me." My eyes fling to hers as they well up with tears. "Remember that time you gave me his number in the bunker? Yeah, well, I called and he acted like the biggest asshole. Told me to stop wasting his time and never call him again."

Mila gasps. "*That motherfucker.*"

I sigh and nod in response. "That was one of those omissions. Turns out the lines were being tapped and he didn't want whoever was listening to know how much I supposedly mean to him."

"Oh, babe. That's fucking horrible. Did you spiral?" I nod once more and her hands immediately go to my shoulders. "I told you to freaking call me!"

"I know." I blink rapidly, trying to keep the tears at bay. "I handled it though, and I'm stronger for it. I just don't know if I'm ready to let him back in just yet."

"Geez. Sounds like you have every right to be skeptical."

I nibble on my bottom lip, gathering the courage to share this next bit.

But unfortunately for me, Mila doesn't give me a chance. "Oh god, there's more, isn't there? I can see it in your face."

"Turns out I got pregnant and then lost the baby, didn't find out until I ended up in the hospital this week."

"Oh god, no! Mel! Was it that bastard Bruce's fault?"

"The doctors think so. Said my HCG levels were there, but they couldn't find a heartbeat. They think the injuries I'd sustained could have caused the loss."

"I'm going to kill him. I'm going to rip off his—"

Just then, Matt enters the kitchen and I beg Mila with my eyes to drop it. I definitely don't want to discuss this in front of any of the Crown brothers.

Thankfully, my best friend nods, but she whispers a promise I try to ignore. "This convo isn't over, girl."

Oblivious to our conversation, Matt moves around the island and the look on his face is not one I care to see so soon after all of the drama we've just had. "Ladies. We need to get going."

"Oh, God, no. Not again," Mila whines and I'm right there with her.

"What now?" I ask, needing more information before my life is uprooted once more.

In answer, Hunter comes up from behind me and I wish I could say it were just his words that have my heart racing. "Catherine has disappeared and we have word that Raul is in Miami. They might be together or there might be another mole. Whatever the case, we need to get the fuck out of here."

I'm blinking up at him, wondering what this all means. "And where would you have us go?"

Without skipping a beat, Hunter takes a step closer, our feet almost touching. "Lake Opalaka."

My breath hitches, the memory of us on the countertop flashing vividly in my mind. Hunter's nostrils flare and jaw clenches. *Oh, he remembers it too.*

"For how long?" My best friend breaks into our moment, but I welcome it—a reprieve from this intensity. "And Jason, he's staying with us, right? He better be staying with us. There's no way in hell I'm letting him traipse across the country with you men. He needs to heal first."

Matt chuckles beside her. "Yes, Mila. He isn't going anywhere that doesn't involve resting and relaxation... well, as much as the situation allows."

"Good. Then it's settled. Ladies, grab your things, we leave in ten." And without even sparing me a single glance, Hunter turns and leaves the room, taking my heart right along with him.

"Uh-huh. You sure you two are done?" Mila bumps my hip with her own.

"Yes, I'm sure." I purse my lips and raise a brow. "Besides, you should be worrying about what you're packing instead of standing here grilling me. Who knows how long this next stint in Colorado will be."

Mila snorts. "Hey, at least we aren't having to go back down into that bunker."

A memory hits me fast and fierce. A looming shadow, the walls of the bunker closing in on me. At first, I think it's Bruce but I hear him in another room, *'This is worth-*

less. Won't get me shit.' The figure above me says something, but it sounds all muffled. I can't make it out.

"Mel! Melissa!" My best friend's hands grip tight around my biceps as she shakes me from my thoughts. "Mel!"

"*Oh, God.* There was someone else. In the bunker…" I'm whispering, trying to beckon the image from the recesses of my mind. I saw them. *I know I did.*

"Someone else? What are you talking about?" Mila's brows push together and her nose scrunches. "Don't you think we should tell the guys?"

This snaps me out of my haze. "No. I'm not telling Hunter anything unless I absolutely have to. Maybe this was a hallucination. Death knocking at my door and ready to take me down with him, right?"

My friend raises a brow, skeptical of my words. "I don't know. Maybe the more time that passes, the more you'll remember."

I nibble on my bottom lip, praying that I either forget all together or remember exactly what happened, because this in between is freaking me the fuck out.

Looking up, I see that Mila isn't sure about this either. "Hey, don't worry about me. I'm going to be okay so long as we get our shit packed in time. Come on. Let's get moving or we'll be forced to wear the same things day in and day out."

Mila cackles. "Oh, heck no. You bet I'd have Hayley delivering the goods in no time."

"Yeah, about that... Remind me to talk to you about her and Matt later on."

Mila stops dead in her tracks, her body whirling around to meet mine. "Girl, you better spill."

I shake my head and laugh. "I will, right after we pack our bags."

Rolling her eyes, Mila gives me a shove. "Fine, but I'm not letting that slide. You're giving me the gossip."

I snicker, knowing there isn't much more than an inkling. But hey, like that saying goes—*where there's smoke, there's fire.*

Hunter

"She's not going to be happy about it," Jace rubs at his scruff, his brow raising in disapproval.

"That's not for you to worry about." I finish checking all of the security cameras in my hub before I turn back toward my brother. "It's in their best interest with you being down for the count and all."

"Hey! I take offense to that. It's not like I wanted to get shot." Jace openly glares, but I don't give a shit.

"Brother, you know better than anyone, if you go into any fight half-cocked and all starry-eyed with emotions, things aren't ending well. You're lucky you're still here with us."

"If you were in my shoes you would've done the same thing."

An involuntary shudder wracks my body. *I don't even want to think about it.* To think of Mel being in a life-threatening situation turns me homicidal.

"Yeah, I'll take your silence as admission." Fucker is back to raising a brow, and this time it's accompanied with a smirk. "So, when are you telling the girls you're leaving us with a babysitter?"

"As soon as he arrives."

Jace cackles. "Oh, brother. You never learn, do you?"

My brows drop and forehead wrinkles. "What are you going on about?"

"Nothing. You'll see soon enough." Jason wheels himself to the study's door but it swings open before he gets to it.

"What is my brother doing here?" My little spitfire knows exactly where to direct her question because her eyes are staring daggers into mine.

"I asked him to come here. Jason isn't in the best shape to keep you safe and I'll be leaving in an hour."

Her mouth drops open, but she quickly shuts it, schooling her features in the process. "Are you coming back?"

There's a hint of vulnerability in her eyes and I'm not sure if now is the time to reassure her. In all honesty, I don't know if I'll be back.

Sure, lying to her will bring her temporary comfort, but

what if I can't keep my promise? Then what? No, it's honesty she wanted and honesty she's going to get.

"I don't know. But it doesn't matter because you'll be safe." I turn toward Ericson who's just entered the room and give him a nod. "Along with your brother, I have several men stationed outside. They'll be rotating on a regular basis, but under no circumstances are you to be alone with any of them. Should you need to talk to them, then your brother and Jace will accompany you. Never, and I mean never, let any of them lure you out of the house without your brother or Jason. Do you understand?"

I see the column of her neck bob with a swallow before she's nodding in agreement. "Fine. But I'm going to need to know you're coming back… just so I can give you shit for putting me in yet another lockdown."

She's trying to be funny, but I see the fear behind her eyes.

"I can't do that, Mel. You wanted honesty, and I honestly don't know if I'll make it home."

Mel's eyes go wide, the crystal orbs going glossy with unshed tears. "Don't say that. Don't you dare say that." She flings herself at me, her small fists pounding against my chest as I hold her tight.

"Shhhh, baby. No matter what, you'll be okay." I thought my words would have a calming effect, but they only serve to agitate her more.

"You big dummy! Don't you get it?" Her eyes bounce back and forth between mine, and I honestly am at a loss for words. "Ugh! For someone so enlightened, you sure do miss the bigger picture a lot."

"Then tell me. Spell it out for my Neanderthal brain." I'm looking down at her, trying to figure it out and praying that she does in fact tell me, because if she doesn't, I'll be forced to pack her up and take her with me. There's no way I'm leaving her in this state.

"Your honesty, I want it when it comes to secrets you hold close to the vest. Secrets that affect you, me, our friends, and our family." Her slender fingers trace my jawline as her eyes look into mine with so much reverence, I may never leave. "You, Hunter Crown, walk around carrying the weight of the world, thinking you know what's best for everyone else. But tell me this? Who is going to look out for you? Who is going to make sure you aren't carrying too much? That what you're holding onto isn't better set free? Who? Tell me who, Hunter?"

My heart, it cracks open, letting enough of her light in, and what I feel is nothing short of a miracle. Warmth. Love. Acceptance. And above all, a soul deep connection. One which gives me a sense of belonging I've never experienced before. *Home.* This woman is my home.

There are no words that could convey what I feel, so I do my best to show her with a kiss, not giving a shit that we have an audience.

Lowering my face to hers, I take her lips in mine, coaxing hers open with my tongue until she's given me access to heaven on earth.

My girl whimpers as I take her tongue, swirling it against mine and savoring everything that is her. Her soft body against my hard one, her warmth against my frigid cold. She's the one I want for the rest of my life; however short it might be. If I had just one more second on this earth, it'd be hers.

Yes, the kiss might have started off as one forged from love and desperation, the need to be closer to her fueling my actions. But it's quickly transformed into nothing but fire and passion, my hips pressing hard against her smaller frame, seeking their home.

I'm about to throw her down and have my way with her, my cock pushing against the zipper of my jeans and needing inside her warm little cunt, but there's a loud slam and it pulls me out of this bubble with Mel.

Fuck. I'd been so lost in her that I'd let the awareness of my surroundings slip.

Letting my ears and eyes refocus on the room around me, I seek out the source of the sound and I find a glaring Ericson.

Unable to help it, I smirk. "Sorry, brother."

Jace snickers. "You're *so* not sorry."

"He isn't," Ericson adds. "But whatever, your ride is here. And thank God. One more second and I swear you would've fucked my sister right in front of me."

"Wouldn't be the first time," Mel mumbles under her breath, her cheeks turning pink as the sweet memories from the bunker come to mind.

"Wait, what?" Jace is looking between all of us but it's Ericson who answers, the green pallor of his face not one I miss.

"You don't want to know. Trust me." Ericson visibly shudders as he swipes a hand over his face. "I still have nightmares."

I raise a brow. "Nothing like the ones you'll have if you don't keep my girl safe while I'm away."

Ericson rolls his eyes. "Whatever. Your ass better get going or that chopper is going to leave without you."

"Another one? Where do you guys keep getting all these helicopters?" Mel is looking between us and the confusion on her face is nothing short of endearing, the sight making me chuckle.

"More secrets, baby. But I promise I'll fill you in as soon as I get back."

She narrows her eyes but the smile playing on her lips lets me know she isn't serious. "You and those secrets, Mr. Crown."

Fuck. Right then and there. That's when I know I need her to be the Mrs. to my Mr. And as soon as I get back, I'm making good on that.

But until then, I'm stealing one more kiss and savoring every second of it, present company be damned.

Chapter Twenty-One
MELISSA

I'M POURING MYSELF A CUP OF COFFEE WHEN MY STOMACH turns and a memory hits me.

'It's still warm, want some?' Bruce's voice is distant, but another one sounds off right above me.

Muffled, but close. I can't quite make it out.

Everything is dark. The only thing I'm able to sense is the smell of coffee wafting near me, that and Bruce's cheap cologne.

"Mel, save some for me." Eric walks into the kitchen, breaking me from the cell my mind has constructed.

It's been two weeks since Hunter left and ever since we

left Florida, bits and pieces of the night down in the bunker have trickled in. But still, I'm unsure if they're something my mind conjured or if it's what actually occurred.

They say trauma has a funny way of messing with your mind and there's no doubt it's definitely fucked with mine.

"Fine. Don't answer. I'll just make some more." My brother scoots past me, his hand reaching up toward a cabinet and pulling out a mug.

He's saying something, but my eyes are trained on the sleeve of his shirt. Bainbridge Valley Turkey Trot, emblazoned in bold letters.

Oh, God... No...

The memory hits me full force.

'No, I don't want any fucking coffee.' *The voice becomes a little bit clearer, but I still can't place it. It's familiar, but my brain isn't working right.*

Struggling, I pry my eyes open and tiny slits of light filter in, sending a shooting pain straight to my brain. Cringing, I shut them again, trying to make sense of the murmurs above me.

'Move! Someone's coming!' *The voice above me shouts, the sudden change in pitch making my eyes shoot open.*

There. Right there on the shadow's sleeve, imprinted in the same bold letters, Bainbridge Valley Turkey Trot.

Pain hits me square in the chest, knocking all air out of my lungs.

"Mel? You okay? You look pale." My brother reaches

for me but I stumble back, needing to make sense of what I just saw.

It can't be, can it? My eyes travel down to Eric's shirt. It's the same color, the same fit, the same black letters.

It's him. He was the looming shadow all this time. He was there when our father beat me. He was there when he got away. Hell, he helped him get away.

But why?

"Mel, you're acting weird." He takes another step toward me, one hand draping over my shoulder. "Here, let's go for a walk. Maybe some fresh air will do you good."

Outside. He's trying to get me outside. All alone.

Over my dead-fucking-body.

Thinking on the fly, I come up with a plan. "Sounds good. Let me put on some boots. I'll meet you by the door in two."

His eyes are narrowed, his expression weary, but he nods in agreement. "Okay. But be quick about it. Don't make me come hunt you down."

I bet you would, brother. I bet you would.

Making haste, I rush toward my bedroom and pull out the burner phone Hunter had given me just before he left. I need to get somewhere private, somewhere Eric won't hear, and tell him everything I've been holding back.

Like a bolt of lightning, a pang of guilt hits me, the hypocrisy of my actions so obvious a blind man could see. How could I expect honesty from my man when I myself have been holding on to these secrets.

No more. As soon as I get to a clearing, I'm telling him everything. Pulling on my boots, I crack open a window and send up a small prayer.

I'm going to need all of the help I can get. My brother is a park ranger and knows these woods like the back of his hand.

Whatever, I still need to try. God knows what'll happen if he knows I've figured him out.

And by some act of grace, I make it to the tree line, breathing easier now that I'll be harder to find inside the thicket.

Yes, I'll be safer, but not in the clear. I just need to make it to the creek. There's a small clearing and I should have enough reception to call Hunter from there.

It seems like forever before I can hear it, the sound of roaring water. Just a few more steps.

"Miss, you shouldn't be out here." A man dressed in camo emerges from behind a tree and I wonder just how long he's been following me for.

I recognize him from the detail that'd been assigned to me, but I'm surprised this is the first I'm hearing from him. My eyes narrow as I look at him head on.

"I've been walking for a good twenty minutes, why didn't you stop me before?"

He nibbles on his bottom lip as his eyes go downcast. "You seemed so sad; I thought you could use the fresh air. But this is far enough. It isn't safe out here and we need to make our way back to the cabin."

What he's saying sort of makes sense, but my nerves are still rattled from my revelation earlier.

Taking my silence as acquiescence, he closes the distance between us, now raising a hand toward the direction where we came from. "After you."

Oh, no. I'm not going with him. Not yet, anyway.

"Sure, right after I make a call." I step around him, continuing on my original path, determined to reach my intended destination. "You're free to follow me if you'd like, but I'm not going back until I've called—"

What the fuck? I haven't even taken two steps when a sharp sting to my neck has my words halting and my brain going all fuzzy. *Oh, shit. Isn't this what happened to Mila?*

Whirling on my feet, I turn to see my attacker. I want to punch him in the nuts, but my body betrays me, dropping to the ground as the branches and leaves form a canopy above me. *God, how I hate this vantage point.* Fuck it. Closing my eyes, I let the darkness take me. At least then I won't feel whatever's coming next.

Hunter

Mel is missing. *Mel. Is. Missing.*

My baby doll. My angel. My home.

"And where the fuck were you when this happened?!" I'm roaring into the line, demanding my brother answer, knowing full well that whatever he says won't be enough.

"I'm sorry, Hunter. I was with Mila. I'd left your girl with Ericson." There's a pause but I don't say anything. I can't. "Look, they're both missing along with another member of the team. It's possible they went off on a walk, not telling anyone else."

Taking in a centering breath, I utter words I'm not sure are much better than the nightmares looping in my head. "Is it possible? Possible, but not likely. Ericson knows better. He knows I'd flip my shit if he didn't inform the team of Mel's location."

"Isn't he still pissed at you? Hell, it sounded like you fucked his sister right in front of him. Maybe he's doing this to get back at you."

My eyes narrow as the thought crosses my mind, yes. This has definitely pissed me right off, but I don't think he'd risk it knowing the hellfire I'd rain down on him.

"No. Something's wrong. I feel it." I run a hand through my hair, the fear inside making me want to rip it right off of my head just so I could feel something else. "Tell me you've grilled the remaining team, that you've already secured reinforcements and called Spencer. Hell, called everyone on that side of the mountain. We need a search party the size of Texas and we need it now."

"Yes to all of it. The men are handing out flyers and we've got canines along with the manpower scouring the woods." He's silent after that, knowing that every second counts in moments like these and it's already been two hours since she was last seen.

If we don't find her soon, we might just never. I don't know for sure who has Mel and her brother, but I have a damn good inkling on who it is.

Based on our surveillance, Raul and Catherine have joined forces, not surprising me one bit. I'm sure that it was *El Jefe's* brother who helped her escape down in Miami.

The question is, how? We still haven't figured that bit out, and a part of me fears that it's the key to unlocking everything.

"Are you on the way, brother?" Jace asks, breaking me out of my thought process and bringing me back to the here and now.

"You know it. Couldn't keep me away." And if by some sick twist of fate, I find that Raul or his henchmen have hurt one hair on my girl's head, then there is no square inch in hell that motherfucker will be able to hide in. I will hunt him down and rip his soul straight out of his body, inflicting torturous pain one pound of flesh at a time.

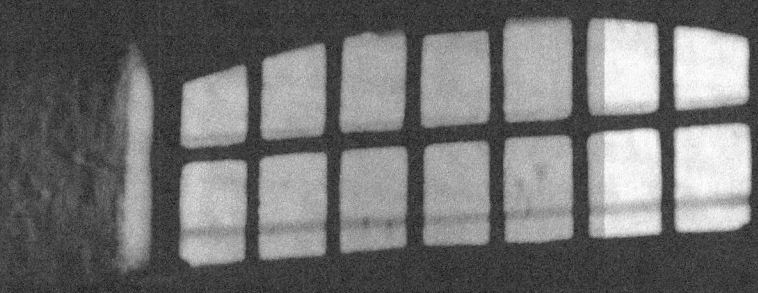

Chapter Twenty-Two
MELISSA

The smell of ammonia has my stomach turning. *Oh god, I'm going to hurl.* Yup, I'm going to hurl.

Needing to get up before I make a mess of myself, I crack an eye open but see nothing.

A sea of black surrounds me, my only company the putrid smell and the distant rattling of chains. *Fuck, this is some straight up horror movie shit.* Where in the hell am I?

I'm almost scared to feel around, unsure of what I'll find. "You've got this, Mel." I whisper to myself in assurance, even though I'm not sure I should be saying anything out loud. God knows if anyone else is around me. Perhaps a monster lurking in the dark, ready to pounce at the first sign of life.

One, two, three... I reach a hand out and feel the ground beneath me. Cobblestone? What is this, a dungeon? Reaching out further, I feel a dip in the ground and a wetness I wish I hadn't touched. It's warm and thick, too thin to be water, but just thick enough to be—

"*Ahhhhh!*"

Something fluttered over my hand as a small squeaking sound rushed past me. "*Holy shit!* Was that a mouse!?"

So much for being quiet.

"Shhh. Keep it down or you'll make him come back." A woman's voice sounds off in the distance, so faint, I wonder if I even heard it.

"Hello? Anyone there?"

"I said shut it," she whisper-hisses, making it clear that I didn't hallucinate her presence. "Do you want to get beat or worse?"

A shiver wracks my body as I remember the last time I got a beat down. Not something I care to repeat.

Even so, I can't stay quiet. We need to find a way out of here and I can't do that without getting more info from my new roommate.

"Hey," I whisper, not wanting to agitate the woman and definitely not wanting to make whoever she's afraid of come back. "I'm Mel, and I don't belong here. Neither do you. If you help me, I promise I'll do whatever I can to get us out."

"*Mel bell.*" the woman croaks, making my entire body freeze in place.

There's only one person who's ever called me that and she abandoned me a long time ago. *It couldn't be, could it?*

Swallowing the lump in my throat, I ask for something I'm too afraid to know the answer to. "I'm sorry. What did you say your name was?"

"I didn't. I don't. We don't need names down here. Apples are for trees and girls are for pews and pies." She starts rambling incoherent phrases I can't quite make out and I think I've lost her.

"Okay... Um, it's just that, the name you called me, Mel Bell, that's something my mother used to call me when I was little." She makes a strangled sound, her incessant chatter finally stopping. "Her name—my mother's name—it was Olivia."

"Olivia, poor Olivia." The woman sniffles, the pain evident in her tone. "She's long gone. Not here anymore."

My heart is beating a mile a minute. "Oh my god, you know of her? She was here? They brought her here?"

"Yes. I knew her. But she's been long gone. Died the moment they took her from her babies."

My heart cracks wide open, immeasurable pain pouring out of me like molten lava. All this time I've blamed her. Thought the worst of her for leaving me and Eric, and she'd been right here, in our town, in this dungeon.

Eric. God, did he do this to her? Couldn't be, he was also just a boy when she'd left.

"Don't cry, Mel Bell. If you stop crying, Mommy will give you some of that chocolate chip ice cream you like so much."

"What?" I choke on a sob. "What did you say?"

"It's your favorite, just like little Eric."

I sit up straight, wiping at my tear-stained face. "And how do you know that?"

She chuckles, "Because you used to beg for it every day after school."

"*Momma?*" My entire body hums with adrenaline, butterflies swimming under every bit of my flesh as I wait for an answer. *It's her. This has to be her.*

"Yes, baby Bell?"

Ohmyfuckinggod. It's her! Full-bodied sobs wrack me as the realization hits me head on. She never abandoned us. She's been trapped in this venerable hell hole this entire time. Our poor mother.

"Shhhh. You have to be quiet or he'll come back. He'll come back and he'll hurt us both."

I shake my head, unwilling to let my brother keep us down here. "Fuck Eric. I'll take him on myself. Punch him in the nuts and make him set us free."

"Ha!" A shiver crawls up my spine as a new voice joins us in the dark. "You think that poor excuse of a man would have the balls to follow in his father's footsteps? Think again, stupid girl."

"Bruce?" I feel my forehead wrinkle as my brain tries to piece this twisted turn of events together.

"No, it's the boogie man. Of course, it's me. Who else do you think could pull something like this off? It sure as fuck isn't your brother."

"But that night in the bunker, there were two of you. I thought that… I thought…"

"You thought… you thought. You can't even string a sentence together, what in the hell makes you think you could figure out who my partner is? I've been running this operation for *El Jefe's* cartel for a good twenty years and to this day, nobody's been able to figure me out." He chuckles, and it's just as well. I need him to keep talking so I can find us a way out of here. I'm feeling around on the ground, searching for something, anything, I need a weapon and I need it now.

Oblivious to my plan, Bruce continues on his rant. "It's a pretty sweet gig if you ask me. I get first use of the girls, getting them nice and ready for transport, and besides, I get to hold on to your momma. I do love her; she's just never learned her place."

It's my turn to laugh, but it's dry and full of sarcasm. "That's not love. It's obsession."

"Love, obsession. It's the same thing." There's a rustling sound and I hear another woman groan. *Jesus, how many of us are there down here?* "Either way, it's something your brother didn't have the balls to handle so I've had to do this all on my own with the occasional help from my silent partner."

This makes my brows furrow; I could've sworn it was Eric. "But I saw him. I saw my brother."

"Well, you sure as shit didn't see Eric. That puny asshole doesn't have the stomach for this." I hear footsteps get closer and I know I'm running out of time. There has to be something I could use. "I tried to teach him when he was little. Show him what a man's supposed to do to his woman, but he just threw up all over his momma. Pathetic little shit."

Just then, a bony hand bumps into mine, the small touch almost making me jump. It's Olivia. I know it is. She must've made her way to me while Bruce was taking us down memory lane.

With a little nudge, she's handing me something, and as I feel for it in the dark, I can sense that it's a homemade shank of sorts. *My god.* She's giving me her weapon.

"Mel Bell. My Mel Bell," she whispers while pushing the blunt edge of the shank into my palm.

"Momma." Closing my free hand over hers, I press mine against her fragile one. *God, I need to get us out of here.*

"Awe. Isn't that sweet. I see you found the woman who baked you." There's some shuffling and a dim light shines through the cavernous space, the vision making me throw up in my mouth.

Bodies. Countless of them. All women, lined against a wall. "Oh my god. Are they…"

"No, child. They aren't worth anything dead. They're

just... *asleep*." Bruce kicks one of the women and she doesn't even flinch. *Shit*. How drugged does he keep them? "They all come and go, but your momma, I keep her around. Service my needs." He licks his lips, and the sight alone has me pitching over to the side, nothing but bile splattering against the dark stone floor.

"Ha! Looks like you and your brother are made of the same cloth. Little bitches. Can't stomach shit." Bruce takes a step closer and Olivia whimpers. *My poor mother.*

No more. As he steps forward, I brace myself, sitting upright and securing the shank I'd hidden underneath my body. It's about time someone put this asshole in his place, and I'm more than happy to be that person.

"Come on, sweetheart. Let's keep it in the family." Bruce's lecherous smile has more bile crawling up my throat, the idea of being with this man in that capacity turning my blood into sludge. "Come and show your father a good time before I send you off to Raul. Turns out you're good for something after all."

Bruce reaches down, fisting my hair as he pulls me up off the ground. *This is it. Now or never, baby doll.*

Maneuvering the shank, I slide the tip between my closed fist and repeatedly punch this sick asshole right in the throat. *One, two. One, two.*

"Sorry. I don't do fathers. Only Daddy's."

"You fucking bitch!" Bruce gargles as he grabs at his throat, blood spurting out meanwhile Olivia's hysterical laughter sounds off behind me.

Fuck, yes! Spurting blood means I must've hit an artery, and it's only a matter of time before he bleeds to death, I just need to make sure he doesn't kill us before then.

But I've spoken too soon, because with a speed that shouldn't be possible, Bruce's hands wrap around my throat and squeeze. I'm trapped, unable to move as he crushes my windpipe, cutting off all air.

I'm thinking all is lost as my vision blurs and I'm gasping for breath, but right then, I hear the sweetest sound —*Bruce grunting in pain.*

"Let my baby go!" Olivia's laughter dies out, replaced by a battle cry of sorts. I don't know what she's doing, but whatever it is it has one of Bruce's hands dropping, giving me the small reprieve I need to stay just shy of death.

Taking the moment for the gift that it is, I lift my knee and crush it against Bruce's nut sack, effectively making him drop the other hand as he bowls over and howls.

Again, he surprises me, recovering way quicker than he should for a man that's bleeding out and on the verge of keeling over.

Like some super freak, he's stumbling toward me, but I'll be damned if I let him catch me or Olivia. Rushing to her side, I lift her off the ground, noticing she's even more frail than I thought. *She's skin and bones.*

"Come on, momma. We gotta get out of here." I rush past a blinking Bruce, his eyes rolling to the back of his head as he starts to convulse. *Finally, Jesus.* It's about damn time the blood loss caught up with him.

"The keys, baby Bell. He has the keys." Olivia mumbles in between bouts of laughter. *Damn it. She's right.*

Looking over at the flailing man I see that he's clutching onto his throat with one hand meanwhile hanging onto a ring of keys with the other. *Bastard.* He may be dying but he knows full well we need those to secure our freedom.

With the little energy he has left, Bruce crawls himself to a drain, his intention painfully obvious. *Oh, hell no.* He's going to throw the keys down that grill, locking us in here until we all die right along with him.

"Not a chance, asshole." I lean Olivia against the wall before I'm flinging myself at my father, my body colliding with his as I reach for his extended hand. "Got it."

I've got it, but Bruce isn't giving in easily. Even in his current state, he's still giving me hell. "Mistake. You were a mistake, stupid girl."

His words hit me deep one last time before there's a loud blast behind me. *Olivia!*

In my haste to reach her, I lose my grip on the keys, the slick metal ring dropping between the slots and disappearing forever. "*Noooo!*"

Bruce's gargled laughter is the last thing I hear before gunshots ring off and I see his body jostle upon impact. *He's done. Gone.* Never to shame me or degrade me again.

I should be looking for gunfire, I should be looking for Olivia, but I'm in a trance, staring at the man who did more damage to my soul than all of my other life experiences combined.

Shuffling feet mix with groans play the soundtrack to my entranced state, the fog only breaking when I hear someone shout behind me. "They're sedated!"

No matter the commotion, I'm still lost in this daze, and it isn't until strong arms wrap around me that I'm detaching my sight from the man at my feet.

"Baby doll, come back to me." Hunter whispers behind me and I finally fall apart, letting everything go in his arms because I'm safe. Safe with a man that's willing to risk his own life and happiness just so I can have my own.

I get it now. Why he's always wanting to carry the weight for those he loves. But too bad for him, I won't let him carry it alone.

Turning back in his arms, I look up into his whiskey-colored eyes and smile. God, he's gorgeous. My man. My Hunter. "Hey, Daddy."

He softly chuckles while shaking his head. "There's my girl. How about we get you home?"

I nod, my eyes finally taking in the rest of the room and seeing that there's a slew of people tending to the multiple bodies. Yes, the sight is tragic, but there's one in particular that makes my eyes prickle and nose sting.

Eric. He's found Olivia, his arms wrapped firmly around her in an embrace. "Momma. I'm so sorry. I should've stopped him. I should've kept him from hurting you."

A knot forms in my throat, the sight too much to bear. I'm shaking now as full-bodied sobs are wrenched from my chest.

"Shhh, baby." Hunter presses his lips to my forehead, trying to calm my nerves, but there's no soothing that'll take this pain away. "It'll be okay. We'll get her home. Promise."

I nod against his mouth, not wanting to detach from this man for a second. There may be no cure for the ache I feel, but this man's touch is the closest thing to it and I'm not planning on letting him go. "I love you, Hunter Crown. So damn much."

"I love you, too, baby doll. You're my world. My everything." And in true Hunter fashion, the man of my dreams picks me up, carrying me bridal style out of this dungeon from hell and into the light, the irony of it all not lost on me.

Three years ago, he did the same. Pulling me out of the darkness I'd been under and carrying me into the light of awareness and enlightenment.

This man has saved me more than once, but it was that very first time that set our destiny in motion, and for that I will forever be grateful. *Grateful for my very own feral Buddha.*

Chapter Twenty-Three
HUNTER

"Is she good?" Jack asks from over his cup of coffee.

"Yeah. Doc looked her over and we're waiting on some labs but she's finally sleeping." I rub at my eyes, wishing like hell that I was in bed right along with her. Unfortunately, there's still some loose ends that need to be tied up.

"Good. She needs it. Hell, can you imagine? It can't be easy finding out that your mother was being held against her will all this time, and by her own husband at that." Jack lets out a low whistle, his head shaking. "About that, how is she doing?"

"She's as good as can be. Eric is with her and we have

the doc running all sorts of test, making sure she doesn't need something we don't have here on hand. So far, she's just got a couple of broken bones and is severely malnourished, but the team is thinking she'll make a nice recovery with time."

"That bastard deserved worse than what he got," Matt mutters under his breath and pride runs through me.

My girl faced her biggest demon and came out on top. Sure, I would've liked to have tortured that sick fuck myself, but I'm glad what transpired was at least able to give Mel some closure, letting her know she held the power all along.

"Don't you worry, brother. There's a special place in hell for scumbags like him. I'm sure of it." Jace sneers, his eyes focused on the hearth's fire.

"Any word on Austin?" Jack asks, placing us back on track with tonight's business.

"No. Last we heard he was in the Appalachian mountains hunting Raul and Catherine down." Matt taps on his phone, his deft fingers typing away at something. "The girls Bruce was running were meant for the cartel which apparently Raul had been running in his departed brother's absence. We think he was going to forward Mel right along with the other girls in his next shipment, not sure if he was aware of the will or not."

Anger clouds my vision as I think of what would've happened had he been successful, but thankfully Jace's words prevent me from going into a full-blown rage. "So the town drunk was just his facade to throw off the authorities. *Bravo*. He did one hell of a job."

"You can say that again," Matt sneers as he pockets his phone. "But that still leaves us with how Catherine fits into all of this. I mean, she's Raul's family. So maybe she's just part of the family business since now she can't show her face in Florida. She knows we'd get after her."

I scoff. "If she thinks she's safer with that homicidal maniac she truly deserves whatever she gets."

Jack *tsks*. "Now, brother. Nobody deserves a Colombian necktie."

I raise a brow in his direction, thinking of the asshole we've just put in the ground.

"My bad. I take that back." He rubs at his lips, his eyes going glossy as he drifts into deep thought. "I say we let the men of WRATH handle this from here on out. This shit has cost our family way too much and I'm not willing to risk losing more than we already have."

My mind flits back to our parents and I know that I will never rest until I've ended all those who cut their life short. "I'm sorry, Jack, but I can't do that. I get that you have a baby on the way, and that your place is here in Colorado, but this is something I have to see through."

He chuckles. "You sound just like Austin. I believe those were pretty much the words he uttered before he disappeared on us."

"And where my womb buddy goes, I go." Matt turns toward me, his brows dropping as the corner of his eyes crinkle. "But if you keep one more secret from me, I'm beating your ass. I don't give a shit if you're two seconds older than me."

"Not two seconds, but okay. No more secrets. Not from me anyway." My words leave the room speechless, the only sound that of the crackling wood. "What?"

Jack answers, "Nothing. We just never thought we'd see the day when you'd finally give up on holding everything down."

Matt comes and claps me on the shoulder. "He's right, brother. It's been a part of you for as long as we can all remember."

"Yeah, well I guess Austin was right. The love of a good woman does have the power to heal."

Jack chuckles. "That it does."

"Ugh. All of you lovesick fools. That shit is for the birds," Matt mumbles as he heads toward the bar before pouring himself some more whiskey.

"Just you wait until that bug bites you, too. You'll be singing a different tune, that's for sure." Jace ribs Matt but I'm pretty sure he's already been bit if his exchange with that boutique girl were any indication.

And as with all things, it'll come crashing into the light with time. Just like my love for Mel. It was built day by day, minute by minute, and there was no amount of suppression or denial I could put down that would keep it from coming to the surface.

In the famous words of Randy Travis, my love is deeper

than the holler, and now that I'm letting myself fully embrace it, there is nothing that could keep me away from my girl.

MELISSA

Soft whispers have me coming out of deep sleep, my body aching as I turn to face the sound. Hunter is by the fireplace, speaking in hushed tones to the family doc.

"Everything okay over there?" I ask, cutting into their moment and catching my man by surprise.

Hunter's eyes are wide, and he looks like the cat that ate the canary. "Okay, somebody better start talking or I'm going to lose my shit."

"Baby doll…" *Oh god, here we go.* He's got that look.

"No more secrets. You promised." I'm pouting, I know I am, but dammit, I thought we were past this.

"No, no secrets. It's just the doctor has some delicate news he has to deliver."

A ball of lead forms in my stomach as I brace for the words. "*Jesus.* It's cancer, isn't it? I have fucking cancer."

"Mel!" Hunter reprimands while the doctor furiously shakes his head.

"No, miss. It's your labs. Everything came back normal with only one particular marker being elevated." He's looking back toward Hunter who gives him a nod, letting him know to continue. "It's your HCG level."

My brows scrunch together and forehead crinkles. "My HCG level?"

"Yes, based on these results, it seems that you may still be pregnant."

My heart jumps into my throat, the thudding so loud I'm surprised nobody else could hear it. "Um, are you sure? Because I was… but then I wasn't."

Hunter squeezes my hand and I see that his eyes are glossy with unshed tears. Damn. He's just as emotional about this as I am.

"I saw that in your chart. It's quite possible that it was too early, and they could've missed something, but we can do a Doppler test right now and check for a heartbeat if you're okay with that?"

My eyes go wide as I turn toward Hunter, his eyes have crinkled at the edges and the most gorgeous smile has graced his lips.

"Okay, yes," I answer the doc but keep my eyes focused on Hunter, all while praying for a miracle.

"Good. Now, Hunter, if you'd please raise her shirt." The doctor shuffles some things in his bag before he's taking out a small tube of jelly and a white piece of plastic with a wand attached. "This is going to be a little cold, but we need to put this on so I'll get a good signal."

I nod, letting him squirt the clear gel onto my stomach before he's turning the device on and pressing the wand to my stomach.

Seconds that feel like hours pass as he moves the long

cylinder along my clammy skin, but then, as if by magic, time stands still and the most beautiful sound I've ever heard graces our ears.

Thud. Thud. Thud.

"Oh my god! Is that?" I'm already in tears as the doctor nods in confirmation, his smile all of the assurance I need. "Our baby! Our little tiny baby!"

Hunter's lips press to the top of my head as his arms wrap around my shoulder. "Jesus. That's the prettiest sound I've ever heard."

With waterlogged eyes, I look up toward my man and smile. "It sure is, isn't it?"

"Congratulations, you two. That's a nice healthy heartbeat." He wipes off my abdomen before placing everything back in his. "I do, however, want to see you in my office sometime this week. We need an official ultrasound just to make sure everything is progressing as it should. But based on the heartbeat and your bloodwork, there's no immediate reason for concern. I say you two rest and enjoy this joyous news."

"Oh, we will, doc. Of that you can have no doubt." Hunter waggles his brows, making the doctor blush.

"Okay, then. I'll leave you two to it." With a speed I'd never seen from him before, he picks up his bag and scurries to the door, not saying another word as he shuts it closed behind him.

"Look what you've gone and done, Daddy. You've scared the poor little doctor."

Hunter chuckles. "Oh, there's only one poor little thing here."

I bite my lip in anticipation, knowing that whatever this man has in mind, it's sure going to be fun. "Oh yeah? And what's that?"

"Your tight little pussy after I've had my way with her." Hunter's mouth descends on my neck and I'm here for all of it. Every last bit of this feral man.

Epilogue
HUNTER

ONE YEAR LATER

"You just love giving my brother a show, don't you?" My girl smirks as I place the picnic basket down on the blanket.

"Hey, he's the one who wanted to come stay with us for the weekend. My friend knows full well I can't keep my hands off of you." I'm raising a brow as I glance over to the lake where Ericson is fishing.

"He wanted to spend time with mom and Livvie, not

get an eyeful of your monster cock." Mel purses her lips to the side, and I can't help but chuckle.

"And what exactly makes you think I'm going to be whipping it out anytime soon?"

Mel pulls the picnic basket open, her gaze accusatory. "Oh, I saw the bag of candy you snuck in there this morning. I knew exactly what you had in mind bringing me out here."

I lick my lips in anticipation, needing my baby covered in marshmallow and chocolate as soon as possible. "I mean, could you blame me? Your mom is watching our daughter, so I get you all to myself. All day every day, those beautiful breasts of yours are like a workhorse, and poor Daddy doesn't even get a lick."

"Poor Daddy, does he need a suckle?" Mel giggles before pulling the neckline of her dress down and exposing the most delicious pair of tits I've ever seen.

She's visibly aroused, the pink tips hard and dripping in anticipation. Instantly, my cock stiffens—but then again there isn't much this woman could do that wouldn't get me ready to take her.

"Yes. Yes, he does." Lowering my body over hers, I let my mouth trail kisses down her neck, over her full cleavage and down onto the pink little nub, already leaking for Daddy.

Like a man starving, I press my soft tongue against the hard little tip, reveling in the mewling noises my baby makes.

"God, that feels so good." Mel wraps her legs around me, rocking her heat into my chest.

I'm lost in the flow of our passion when I hear it—Ericson bellowing in the distance.

"Goddammit, you two! Can't even go fishing without you guys going at it like fucking rabbits."

I chuckle against my baby's full tit, giving it a tender nibble before I let go. "If you think this is bad, then you need to get going because it's about to get a whole lot worse."

"*Motherfucker.*" I hear him grumble behind us, the sound of feet shuffling away following right after.

"Oh, God. I can't believe you let him watch that." Mel blushes but I know she likes a little bit of voyeurism. There's no denying it gets her wetter faster.

"As long as nobody sees this," I lower a hand and lift the hem of her dress, giving her tight little cunt a slap, "then I don't have a problem with it. Because *this*," I slide two thick fingers underneath the already damp lace, gliding them up and down along her swollen lips, "*it's for me and only me.*" I growl as I shove myself deep inside, reveling in the way Mel's eyes roll back in her head. She's panting, hungry for more as I slowly thrust in and out.

"That's right, baby. Who makes you feel good?"

"You do, Daddy. Only you." Mel rolls her hips against my hand, her seductive moves casting a spell over me as her engorged breasts beg for another suckle, to which I gladly oblige.

My hot mouth wraps around the fleshy mound, my tongue lapping at the sweet liquid dripping like mana from the sky.

"Mmmph, more. Give me more." Mel's pussy pulses around me, her movement becoming erratic as she seeks relief.

My greedy little girl.

I let her voluptuous tit fall from my mouth as a slow and wicked grin forms on my lips. "Is my baby going to be good or bad?"

Mel laughs, her head falling back as her chest sways before me.

"Good. I'll be good, Daddy."

I wink, knowing she doesn't want the torture and wants to skip right to the pleasure. "Fine. But that doesn't mean I won't get to play a little."

Mel's jaw drops as I pull out the bag of candy, a long lollipop firmly gripped in my hand.

"*Oh my god.*"

She said she wanted to be good, but I see the way her pupils dilate.

Bringing the swirled confection closer to her face, I let the blunt tip run over her lips, loving the way her chest rapidly rises and falls.

"Such a good girl." I nudge the candy forward, my brow raising in command. "Open that pretty mouth for Daddy."

Her eyes glass over with lust as she does what I say,

and without hesitation I shove the candy deep inside, growling out my demand. "Now suck. Suck it good and hard."

Once more, my good girl does what I ask, my cock pulsing in response.

I'm a leaking throbbing mess in my jeans, watching as my baby sucks and swirls around the fucking candy I wish so desperately were me.

"Jesus, baby. That fucking mouth." In one swift move, I shove my pants down, pulling out my hard length before I'm letting it take the lollipop's place. "*Fuuuuuuck.*"

My girl doesn't miss a beat, taking my turgid flesh in her mouth, sucking me in until I'm balls deep in that tight little throat. Like a pro, her hands go to my ass, pushing me in further before pulling me out, and it takes everything in me not to nut on the spot.

Looking down I see her eyes tear up, the gagging sounds she makes with every thrust forward like music to my ears.

"So good, baby. You suck Daddy's cock so good." My hand strokes down her head, fingers digging deep into her hair before I'm giving two hard thrusts and releasing my hold. "But I think it's time my girl got her reward, don't you?"

Mel nods as my thumb swipes her fat bottom lip.

"Question is, what does she want?"

Slender fingers wrap around my fat girth and stroke, my

girl knowing exactly what to do to make me putty in her hands.

Mel lets her free hand trail over both breasts before giving each a squeeze, "I need your mouth here," she moans, her other hand continuously working me while the other drops lower to the apex of her thighs, "and your cock here."

She slaps at her pussy, the visual of it sending a rogue spurt of cum shooting onto her creamy tits.

"Christ, woman. You make me fucking mad."

"Awe, poor Daddy." She urges me lower, nudging her slick entrance with my swollen head, teasing it with heaven on earth. "Does he need his baby's tight little cunt?"

And with a raise of her hips, my girl is impaling herself on my length, the one move making my eyes roll back as a bolt of lightning tingles down my spine.

Holy shit, she feels good.

Roaring into the sky, my hands go to her hips as I rut into her without mercy.

"Fuck, baby. You're gonna take it. *Take it like the good girl you are.*" I thrust into her repeatedly, never slowing my pace as I watch her full tits bounce with every push forward. No, this isn't tender or sweet. It's feral fucking, and I know my baby wouldn't have it any other way.

She and I, we share a soul, our jagged edges fitting around each other and making the other whole.

No, there's nothing conventional about our love, but

normal is overrated. And as my girl shudders and shakes, I know that I'll do whatever it takes to keep it safe, even if it costs me my dying breath.

Thank you for taking a chance on Feral Crown! If you enjoyed it, please consider leaving a review here. They help me out tremendously and I'd greatly appreciate it.

MEN OF WRATH

Acts of Atonement: A Single Dad Age Gap Romance

Acts of Salvation: An Age Gap Romance

Acts of Redemption: A Second Chance Romance

Acts of Grace: A Brother's Best Friend Romance

Acts of Mercy: A Stepbrother Romance

CROWN BROTHERS

Filthy Crown: A Single Dad Age Gap Romance

Trojan Crown: A Single Dad Age Gap Romance

Sinful Crown: A Single Dad Age Gap Romance

ACKNOWLEDGMENTS

This is always the hardest bit for me to write. There are so many people that helped this book be the best it could be and I feel that paltry words of gratitude are never enough.

Lauren and Suny, I thank you each and every time because you two are the peanut butter to my jelly. I am beyond grateful for all of the time you've shared; reading, making edits, and telling me where I've dropped the ball. You ladies are the real MVPs and I appreciate you to the moon and back.

A huge thank you also goes out to Mary with OnPointe-Digital Services. She's an amazing human with amazing work ethic. Thank you for speed-reading this baby on short notice and for helping me catch all of the little tidbits I missed. You're the best!

I'd also like to thank Salina, Kristien, and everyone else on the ARC team. You ladies are rockstars, and I am over the moon with all of the feedback you've shared. That paired with the amazing edits you share, you're all such a big part of this release. Thank you a million times over.

And last, but of course not least, thank you. Thank you for choosing my book baby. There are thousands upon thousands of books out there, and you chose mine. I only hope that it was an enjoyable journey and that it was one that'll keep you coming back for more. Sending you all of my love and gratitude—always.

www.ingramcontent.com/pod-product-compliance
Lightning Source LLC
LaVergne TN
LVHW010312070526
838199LV00065B/5531